ABOUT THE A

Michael Coleman was born in Forest Gate,
East London. In his life journey from aspiring
footballer to full-time writer he has variously been
employed as a waiter, a computer programmer,
a university lecturer, a software quality assurance
consultant and a charity worker. He is married,
with four children and one grandchild.

Michael has written many novels, including the
Carnegie Medal shortlisted *Weirdo's War*. His website
can be found at www.michael-coleman.com

The Howling Tower is the first gripping title in
The Bear Kingdom trilogy. Look out for the subsequent
titles – *The Fighting Pit* and *The Hunting Forest*.

Acclaim for *Weirdo's War*:

'Tense, psychological and instructive.' *The Times*

As thought-provoking as it is exciting...addresses
fundamental truths about human character
and behaviour.' *Booktrusted News*

501 112 587

In memory of Tony Pickup (1936–2005)

ORCHARD BOOKS
338 Euston Road, London NW1 3BH
Orchard Books Australia
Hachette Children's Books
Level 17, 207 Kent Street, Sydney, NSW 2000, Australia

ISBN 1 84362 938 0

First published in Great Britain in 2006
A paperback original
Text © Wordjuggling Limited 2006
The right of Michael Coleman to be identified as
the author of this work has been asserted by him in
accordance with the Copyright, Designs and Patents Act, 1988.
A CIP catalogue record for this book is available from the British Library.

1 3 5 7 9 10 8 6 4 2
Printed in Great Britain

THE BEAR KINGDOM

THE HOWLING TOWER

MICHAEL COLEMAN

ORCHARD BOOKS

CONTENTS

WHAT IF...?

Everybody knows that crazy humans have battled with other crazy humans ever since they grew – well, crazy enough to fight battles.

But not so many people know that the biggest and longest battle fought by we humans was against another species altogether: the cave bear. For several hundred thousand years our ancestors battled with these bears for the right to live in the caves that would shelter them from freezing weather and keep them away from sharp-toothed animals looking for something juicy and two-legged to eat.

Fortunately for us, this war was won by the humans. Unfortunately for the cave bears, they died out long ago.

But what if the cave bears had won...?

BENJAMIN WILDFIRE

Benjamin Wildfire had decided to run away. He knew it would be the most dangerous thing a young human could possibly try, but Benjamin's mind was made up. He couldn't put up with the cruel Mrs Haggard any longer.

Mrs Haggard was Benjamin's owner. She was a thin, bony bear who couldn't forget that she'd once been beautiful. Mrs Haggard would look back on those days – when her fur had been silky and her huge, rounded bottom had swayed wondrously from side to side as she padded along the road – and wish with all her heart that there was a way of recovering her youthful good looks. Because of this she spent most of her money on lotions and potions that were supposed to do just that.

There was very little money left over to buy anything else, least of all decent food for Benjamin Wildfire. He had to make do with bowls of scraps and the occasional treat that Mrs Haggard might toss his way when she was in a good mood (which wasn't very often). Benjamin was fed up with always feeling hungry.

He was even more fed up with regularly being cuffed round the ear for no reason at all, while Mrs Haggard bellowed at him names like:

'Snout-point!'

'Bum-fluff!'

'Claws-blunt!'

Mrs Haggard had almost as many nasty names for Benjamin as she had lotions and potions for herself. But her absolute favourite was:

'Sap-squeak!'

This insulting name needs explaining. First, the 'sap' part. This comes from something that bears are taught from cub-hood – that humans are commonly known as saps. Mrs Haggard remembered her teach-bear saying that the word came from the Ancient Bear-Language term *sapiens-homo*, meaning 'thinking man'. How the whole learn-class laughed when they heard that their forebears once believed that humans could think!

Now the 'squeak' part. Bears – even nasty old females like Mrs Haggard – have very deep voices. To them, human speech sounds like nothing more than lots of high-pitched squeaks, not that much different to the noises made by flocks of twittering birds.

Putting the two parts together made 'sap-squeak', which Mrs Haggard thought was very clever. Whenever she said it she growled with laughter.

Not so Benjamin Wildfire. He had nothing to laugh about. He hated being hungry, and cuffed round the ear, and bellowed at. But, even more than these, Benjamin hated spending all day, every day, in the dark and dingy den that Mrs Haggard called home.

The days when the bears had lived in real caves were long gone. They had discovered how to make outside dens from clay and wood and other materials they could shape with their amazing claws. Mr Haggard had been very clever in this regard. In the days when he'd been alive the den had looked quite smart. The outside of the large, solid dome had been a delightful burnt orange colour. Now it was a filthy shade of mud-brown and its once strong, teak doors were slowly being rotted by layers of green mould.

Things were no better inside. The eating-chamber hadn't been washed in years. The walls of the cooking-chamber were covered in so much grease that on hot days it would melt and dribble down to make a puddle on the floor. And as for the plopping-chamber...well, the least said about that the better.

Only in Mrs Haggard's sleeping-chamber was there the slightest hint of comfort. This contained a large wooden bed with a soft, leaf-filled mattress and an enormous stone table upon which was laid out the vast collection of lotions and potions that was supposed to keep Mrs Haggard looking fat and fabulous.

Needless to say, Benjamin Wildfire wasn't allowed to set foot in any of these chambers. He was expected to spend most of his days and all of his nights curled up by the back door...with his chain curled up beside him.

Yes, his chain. The moment she'd brought Benjamin home, Mrs Haggard had attached a heavy iron chain to his ankle and secured it to the wall beside the back door with an even heavier iron padlock.

'Hear-me you climbing-clever,' Mrs Haggard had laughed nastily. 'Well, not-you over-get my fence-back!' (She often spoke aloud like this to Benjamin, even though she *knew* he didn't understand her.)

Mrs Haggard wasn't completely heartless, though. The chain was a long one. Long enough to stretch from Benjamin's place near the back door all the way along the gloomy passageway to the front door. Long enough, also, for Benjamin to clank from the back door down to the bottom of Mrs Haggard's garden when he was allowed out.

These outings took place shortly after sun-come and again shortly before sun-go. 'Business-do!' Mrs Haggard would order, opening the back door and shoving him out. 'Quick-be!'

But, far from being quick, Benjamin always tried to make his trips into the small garden last as long as possible. He did this for three reasons.

The first reason was that these were the only times he ever left the den. Mrs Haggard never took him out with her, however straight Benjamin sat or appealingly he smiled.

'Stay-you here,' Mrs Haggard would say before leaving him. 'Got-me you for guard-sap not pet-sap!'

So, whenever the scraggy old she-bear went out, Benjamin was meant to stay inside and keep his ears and eyes open. If he heard or saw anything unfamiliar he was expected to shout and holler and scream at the top of his voice to warn the whole street.

This made simply getting out of the den and into the fresh air the first reason Benjamin loved going into the garden so much.

The second reason was because it reminded him of happier days.

That's not to say it was a gorgeous garden, dripping with fruits and glowing with flowers. It wasn't. It was full of tall weeds and brambles and the dry remains of long-dead trees and bushes. Mrs Haggard spent too long pampering her furry face to spend any time working in her garden.

So why did it remind Benjamin Wildfire of happier days? To explain this, we will have to travel back in time — to just five summers after Benjamin was born.

Together with his father, Duncan, and his mother, Alicia, Benjamin was living on a fruit farm. Their owner was a short-sighted he-bear who fed them well and treated them kindly. Even the name-collar he'd put round Benjamin's neck was made of the softest material he could find.

Benjamin was allowed to run about and climb high into the fruit trees from sun-come to sun-go. Then, worn out and blissfully happy, he'd snuggle onto his father's lap and listen to the magical stories he told. Benjamin's favourite had always been one about a place called Hide-Park. According to his father, this was a wonderful land where saps roamed free and nobody ever chained them up or told them what to do. He'd always ended the story with the same words: 'One sun-come we'll all be there together, Benjamin.'

But those carefree times had come to an end. Too frail to work any more, the old bear sold his fruit farm to new owners. Almost at once, strange bears began turning up to inspect Benjamin. They looked in his mouth and waggled his limbs and poked his body in places they had no right to poke. They nodded approvingly at his glowing, good health; they were pleased to see his bright, alert eyes. But then they looked again at Benjamin's bright red hair and shook their heads. Bears are very wary of fire, you see. They conquered it thousands of moons ago and they use it now for everything from melting metals and making glass to cooking their chewier foods and warming their dens, but they know how extremely dangerous it is. Saps with fiery hair, goes the common belief, mean trouble!

This hadn't bothered Mrs Haggard in the slightest. Quite the opposite. She'd jabbed a sharp claw in

Benjamin's soft, pink backside, and when he let out a piercing shriek of angry pain she exclaimed delightedly: 'Full-wonder! Want-me sap-fiery!'

She'd handed over a round (which is what bears call the metal discs they use for buying things), then carried little Benjamin away from his tearful parents. He hadn't seen them since.

And that, to get back to where we were, is the second reason why Benjamin Wildfire loved roaming around and climbing (as much as his chain would allow) the old trees in Mrs Haggard's jungle-like garden. Out there, he could pretend he was breathing free air. He could pretend there wasn't a chain round his ankle and that he was exploring a wonderful new world. In other words, Benjamin could pretend that he'd found the fabulous Hide-Park of his father's bedtime stories. And he could dream that one day he would escape from Mrs Haggard's chain and head off in search of Hide-Park itself...

So, finally, we come to the third reason that Benjamin Wildfire looked forward to his daily trips to the bottom of the garden. He had found, under the weeds and bracken, a large and jagged lump of stone. After doing his business one gloomy morning he'd trodden on it and cut his bare foot quite badly.

Mrs Haggard had been unsympathetic. She'd done nothing more than give the injury a quick lick.

'Whining-stop!' she'd snapped. 'Got-you foot-another.'

The accident had made Benjamin think, though. If

that stone could cut into his foot, then perhaps it could cut into other things – like chains.

And so, out of Mrs Haggard's sight, Benjamin would sit down beside that stone. He would gather together the section of chain closest to his ankle and rub the same link against the stone's jagged edge.

Rub, rub, rub.

Garden outing after garden outing.

Rub, rub, rub.

Until the memorable day that the link gave a little ping – and snapped.

MOPS

Nearly thirty sun-comes had passed since Benjamin had cut through the link on his chain and been able to release himself whenever he wanted. All that time he'd been preparing. Now, he was almost ready to make his escape bid.

Benjamin had known there was no point in making a run for it without taking some food to live on. And so, hard as it had been from the miserable helpings Mrs Haggard gave him, at every meal time Benjamin had sneaked some food into his pockets instead of his mouth.

He'd also managed to snaffle some extras. Whenever Mrs Haggard went out (to have her fur clipped, for example) Benjamin would remove the link from his chain and set himself free. First, he would spend a little while dancing and jumping for joy at the sheer delight of not having the heavy chain dragging behind him. Then he would head for Mrs Haggard's food-nook. There he'd take a handful to add to his store. As he'd not been greedy, Benjamin had been able to build up a small hoard of food without Mrs Haggard being any the wiser.

This hoard was hidden at the bottom of the garden (well away from where Benjamin did his business, I might add!). Every time he sneaked some more food out in his trouser pockets he'd bury it quickly, before Mrs Haggard called him back in. It was while he was doing this – on the morning our story really begins – that Benjamin heard the voice.

'What *are* you doing?'

Benjamin swung round, startled. He heard a giggle. Then, above the rickety, wooden fence which divided Mrs Haggard's garden from that of her next-den neighbour, he saw a face. A girl's face.

A highly decorated girl at that. Her fair hair had been plaited with ribbons and sprinkled with flowers of berry pink. Her fluffy dress had been dyed berry pink. Her legs and feet, had Benjamin been able to see them from his side of the fence, were clad in the same colour. Even her underwear (which he *definitely* couldn't see) was berry pink.

'Who are you?' gasped Benjamin.

The girl sniffed. 'My name is Millicent Ophelia Patience Snubnose.'

'Blimey,' muttered Benjamin (who, until then, had thought that Benjamin Wildfire was a long name).

'You may call me Mops, for short. That's what my owner does.'

'Mops?'

The girl pointed at her pink name-collar. 'M for Millicent, O for Ophelia—'

'I get it,' Benjamin interrupted rudely.

This rudeness was nothing at all to do with Benjamin being red-haired and fiery. He simply wanted to hide his latest food snafflings before being called in by Mrs Haggard. At the same time, he didn't want this Mops girl to see any more than she already had. She was obviously a pet-sap and from the way Mrs Haggard talked he got the impression that most pet-saps were lazy nothing-for-goods. But if this one was the curious sort it could ruin all his plans.

Unfortunately, she *was* the curious sort. 'You still haven't told me what you're doing,' she said.

'Nothing. Go away.'

Mops sighed. 'Typical boy. All silly secrets and digging holes. Shall I *tell* you what you're doing, then? You're hiding food. You've been doing it for almost a moon. And shall I tell you *why* you're hiding food? Because you're planning to run away!'

'Ssssshhh!' cried Benjamin, his eyes nearly popping out of his head. 'If my owner hears you...'

Mops dismissed the objection with a waggle of a regularly-washed hand. 'Pah! You know she wouldn't understand a word we're saying.'

Benjamin knew this was true. Humans can understand what bears say, but bears – even though many of the words they use are the same – simply can't understand humans. This isn't only because human voices sound squeaky to them. It's also because a bear's brain works far more slowly than a human's. Now and again they might think their sap has uttered a word they recognise, but quickly making sense of lots of their words joined together is completely beyond them.

'Still,' Mops went on, 'if it makes you any happier, I'll whisper. You *are* planning to run away, aren't you?' she whispered.

'I might be,' shrugged Benjamin.

'I would if I were you and I'd managed to break my chain,' said Mops airily.

Horrified, Benjamin looked down at his chain. In full view of this nosey pet-sap it had come unlinked.

Mops sounded impressed, though. 'You are clever! I'd never have thought of that.'

Benjamin quickly linked his chain back together. Any moment now Mrs Haggard would be bellowing for him to come in. Ignoring Millicent whatever-her-name-was he pulled his food bag out from its hiding place and added his latest collection to it.

'Well that lot won't last you long,' trilled Mops, leaning over the fence to get a better look. 'You'll starve before you reach the end of the road!'

'No, I won't,' snapped Benjamin.

'Well I *certainly* will,' Mops snorted irritably. She sighed grandly. 'I can see I'm going to have to bring more provisions than I anticipated. And I don't suppose for an instant you've thought about packing the other *essentials* of life – a hair brush, nail varnish, clean underwear...'

'Wh-what?'

'Well don't just sit there gawping,' said Mops. 'When do we leave?'

'*We*? You mean you want to run away as well?' said Benjamin, staring at Mops's beautifully groomed hair and freshly scrubbed face. 'But – why?'

'Because I am *bored*! Bored, bored, bored! Do you have the slightest idea what it's like to be a pet-sap and spend your whole life flopping around on cushions and being scratched behind the ears?'

Benjamin, who knew nothing about cushions and only about being thumped behind the ears, didn't have a chance to reply.

'Well I can tell you it is *totally boring* and I can't stand it any longer! I want to see the whole wide world and have really exciting adventures!'

'So...you're saying...you want to run away? With... me?'

Mops clapped her hands. 'He's there at last! Give the boy a biscuit! Yes, I want to run away with you. Now, when do we make the big break?'

Mrs Haggard chose that moment to roar from the back door. 'Benjamin Wildfire! Here-come, before-me alive-you-skin!'

'Well?' hissed Mops as Benjamin scrambled to his feet. 'When do we go?'

'Late tomorrow,' Benjamin hissed back quickly. 'After sun-go.'

'Goody goody!' squeaked Mops. 'I'll start packing at once!'

Benjamin didn't wait to say goodbye. Holding his chain tightly in position to make sure the broken link didn't show, he turned and scurried back to where Mrs Haggard was waiting.

Yes, he thought as he ran, the best time would be when the sound of Mrs Haggard's snoring would tell him that she was in the deepest of deep sleeps. But – he wasn't going to wait until after tomorrow's sun-go. His conversation with Mops had made his mind up about that. Being on the run was going to be dangerous enough without having an irritating girl for company.

No, decided Benjamin. He was going to run away in an earlier darkness: in the darkness just before tomorrow's sun-come.

NIGHT FLIGHT

Peering out through the small round murky window in the front door of the den, Benjamin watched the moon grow brighter and the sky grow darker. He saw the stars appear, sparkling more than even the sparkliest of Mrs Haggard's jewels. Perfect. He sat down and waited.

Eventually he heard a shuffling outside. Dutifully, and carefully holding his chain in place, Benjamin leapt to his feet and began to yell at the top of his voice. If proof were needed that bears didn't understand humans it came at moments such as this, because what he actually yelled was: 'Go away, you skinny old bear-bag!'

And what did Mrs Haggard say as she came in? 'Sap-good! Nice and noisy-loud!' Her pleasant mood quickly returned to normal, though. Cuffing Benjamin round the head she growled, 'Now corner-go!'

'Just as you say, Your Ugliness,' Benjamin muttered. 'Because it's going to be the last time ever!'

He curled up, pretending to be guarding dutifully, while through narrowed eyes he watched every move that Mrs Haggard made. He watched her tuck in to a heavy meal of berries and acorns, washed down with a jugful of water. Then he saw her shuffle into her sleeping-chamber, and heard the guzzling of potions and sloshing of lotions as Mrs Haggard went through her sun-go beauty rituals. Finally, Benjamin heard the scrunch of her leaf-filled mattress and knew that his owner had settled down for the night.

He didn't sleep. Neither did he move, until he judged that sun-come was close. By then, he knew also that Mrs Haggard was sleeping soundly, for a rumble was echoing round the walls like rolling thunder. To be quite sure, Benjamin wriggled down the passageway on his front until he was able to peep into Mrs Haggard's sleeping-chamber. The old bear's scraggy hide was rising and falling in rhythm with the noise. Yes, she was snoring. It was time!

Silently unlinking his chain, Benjamin carefully laid it aside and stood up. All he had to do now was ease open the back door and run to the bottom of the garden to dig up his supplies. Then he'd scramble over the back fence and be off as fast as he could go. But first...

Benjamin picked up the end of his chain for one last time. Then carefully − oh, so carefully − he carried it into Mrs Haggard's sleeping-chamber. There, he wound the chain tightly round one of the stone table's four stone legs. Then, pulling it taut across the doorway, and just off the ground, Benjamin tiptoed down the passageway and looped the chain's other end round the heavy front-door knob.

'Gggggrrrrrmmmpphhh!' snorted Mrs Haggard, turning restlessly in her bed.

Worried in case she wasn't sleeping as deeply as usual, Benjamin knew he could wait no longer. Easing open the back door, he slipped silently into the night.

By the strong glow of the moon, Benjamin crept swiftly down to the bottom of the garden. Quickly he retrieved his supplies. Now to start climbing! Up he leapt, only to have a cloud choose that moment to float in front of the moon. Unable to see where he was going in the sudden darkness, Benjamin stumbled into the wooden back fence with a loud thump.

On any other night this might not have mattered. When Mrs Haggard was in one of her deepest sleeps you could have thumped a wooden back fence right beside her ear and she wouldn't have stirred. But this was not one of those nights. On this night, of all nights, Mrs Haggard wasn't sleeping well. She was in the middle of an awful dream.

For some reason the King's army was hunting for old and scraggy bears. 'Bears-old are bears-useless!' they were shouting as they marched down the street outside. In her dream she'd been expecting them to pass her by, but they hadn't. They'd stopped right outside her den. They were coming for her! Now they were breaking her door down. She could hear them thumping hard on the wood...

Waking up in a terrible fright, Mrs Haggard had immediately realised that she'd been dreaming. There was no army trying to break down her door. But in that case...where had the very real sound of wood being thumped come from? And why hadn't Benjamin Wildfire raised the alarm?

Lumbering bleary-eyed from her bed, Mrs Haggard poked her head out of her sleeping-chamber window. It looked out on the garden – which was how, as the moon chose that very moment to reappear, she saw Benjamin Wildfire hadn't raised the alarm The wretched sap was trying to escape!

'Snivelling sap-squeak!' bellowed Mrs Haggard. 'Here-come!'

Fully intending to drag Benjamin back inside by his fiery red hair, Mrs Haggard galloped towards the doorway as quickly as her four old legs would carry her – only to blunder straight into Benjamin's carefully positioned chain. As the stone table was dragged over, lotions and potions flew into the air, then splattered down on the entangled Mrs Haggard's head.

'Benjamin Wildfire!' she howled. 'Wish-you never-born will! Going-me to apart-you-tear!'

Out in the garden, Benjamin knew he had no time to lose. The noise Mrs Haggard was making would soon have the whole street awake. Scrambling over the fence, he dropped down to the alleyway which ran behind all the back gardens.

Where now, though? Benjamin looked both ways. To his left, he could see hardly anything. The alley just seemed to disappear into the inky darkness. But to his right, away at the far end of the alley, he could just make out what looked like a blazing torch attached to a tall post. That had to be the best way to go. Clutching his bag of supplies, Benjamin turned to his right – and ran!

The alley was smelly and slippery. Rocks and stones littered the ground, slowing him down. As he ran, Benjamin looked back anxiously to see if Mrs Haggard was chasing after him. She wasn't. Even better, her roaring seemed to be growing fainter. By the time he reached the torch-post at the end of the alleyway, it had died completely.

Benjamin skidded to a halt. Holding his breath, he peered out. The torch-post he'd been aiming for wasn't the only one. There were lots of them, spaced out along the length of a wide, flat strip of ground. Extra light was also coming from the curious dens which lined both sides of this flat-way. Quite unlike Mrs Haggard's den, these had illuminated fronts behind which all kinds of articles were on display. Interesting as this was, Benjamin was much more excited by another feature of these dens: each one had a shadowy doorway, perfect for hiding in while you thought about what to do next. Spotting one just a couple of paces away from where he was, Benjamin darted out of the alley and leapt into the shadows.

He was just in time. No sooner had he tucked himself out of sight than he heard a strange bumbling, rumbling sound.

It was coming from the alley he'd just left. And it was getting closer. Benjamin flattened himself even further into the doorway. Faster and nearer came this strange rumbling sound, until it stopped right next to where he was hiding.

Then an irritated voice said, 'Well, *really*! If I remember rightly, you said you were going to run away *tomorrow* sun-go! It's a good job I was packed and ready, that's all I can say!'

And into the doorway, dragging a rumbling, spangly wheeled box behind her, flounced Millicent Ophelia Patience Snubnose (Mops for short).

THE UNDER-TOWN

Benjamin groaned. That this nosey girl-next-den had followed him was bad enough. But to have done so, bringing with her whatever she had, was *awful*. Even in the gloom of the doorway its spangled wheels were glittering and glinting. And, on top of that, it was huge.

'How do you expect to stay out of sight with that thing?' he hissed.

'This is not a *thing*,' replied Mops icily. 'This is a wheely-box. Used only by the most superior sap-pets to carry supplies for their owners.'

'What in Bear Kingdom have you got in it?'

'Everything I could think of that might prove useful.'

'You must have thought of a lot of things,' snapped Benjamin.

'Of course. Thinking of things is what I'm best at. Which is just as well,' Mops said as she wagged her finger under Benjamin's nose, 'because if it hadn't been for my thinking, you'd be back in Mrs Haggard's chains already!'

'What!' The mere mention of his owner's name had started Benjamin quivering again.

'When I heard all the noise she was making I knew what you must be up to. So I hurried out with my bits and pieces, just in time to see you race past our back gate. Anyway, that's when I also saw your owner dragging herself out into the garden. And did she look a mess, all covered in gooey stuff!'

'Lotions,' said Benjamin.

'Well, whatever they were, she was *angry*! No climbing over the fence for her, she started tearing it down with her bare paws! So I thought to myself: Mops, you'd better do something to get her going the wrong way. So I did.'

'You did?' said Benjamin, agog. 'What?'

'Simple. I just lobbed a few stones over the fence in the direction I knew you *hadn't* gone. The noise fooled her completely. In an instant that poor fence was in bits and she was lumbering off towards the scratching-tree square. You did know that's what's at the other end of our alley?'

Benjamin shook his head thoughtfully. He hadn't known that. In fact, the more he talked to Mops the more it seemed he didn't know. Perhaps having her with him wouldn't be such a bad idea after all, even with her wheely-box in tow.

'Right!' said Mops brightly, 'where are we going?'

That, Benjamin did know. 'Hide-Park. My mother

and father used to tell me stories about it. It's a place where saps are free to do just what they like.'

'Ooh! That sounds wonderful! So, which way is it?'

Benjamin shrugged. 'I don't know,' he said softly.

'You don't know?' squawked Mops. 'You mean you haven't got a route to this place worked out?'

Benjamin shook his head. 'I don't even know for sure that it exists.'

'Oh, brilliant! I've run away with a boy who doesn't know which way he's running!' She peered out from the doorway. The sky was getting lighter. 'Well we can't stay here. It will be the crush-hour soon.'

'The crush-hour?' echoed Benjamin.

'The time when all the work-bears go off to their jobs,' said Mops. 'My owner never liked taking me out at that time. Too busy, she always said.'

'Mrs Haggard never took me out at any time,' said Benjamin. 'That's why I don't know where to go now.'

Mops gripped the handle of her wheely-box and stepped boldly out of the doorway.

'Then you'd better follow me, hadn't you?' she sighed. 'I don't suppose you can read, either?'

Benjamin's eyes opened wide. 'You mean you *can*?'

'Quite a bit. My owner taught me. She liked to show me off to her friends. She'd write down silly instructions like "tummy-tickle" and "ear-scratch" and I'd obey them. Well, it kept her happy. Didn't Mrs Haggard teach you any tricks?'

31

'Only how to make loud, frightening noises.'

'Oh, that *will* come in useful,' snorted Mops, 'I don't think!'

'It might...'

But Mops wasn't listening. She was already marching quickly away, her wheely-box rumbling and twinkling behind her. Benjamin hurried to catch up.

'Where are we going?' he hissed.

'We have to get out of sight quickly, before the crush-hour begins,' said Mops without stopping. 'If saps are caught without their owners they're taken away, that's what I've heard.'

'I've heard that, too,' said Benjamin.

Mrs Haggard had regularly muttered to herself that she'd hand him over to a mysterious Sap-Catcher if he didn't do his job properly. Benjamin had never found out exactly what Sap-Catchers did with saps, only that falling into the claws of one was *not* a good idea.

'Not just out of sight, though,' continued Mops, thoughtfully. 'We've also got to get much further away from our owners.'

This sounded very confusing. 'How can we get out of sight *and* away?'

Mops sighed and pointed. 'There.'

Just ahead of them a large cave with a sign above its entrance. This sign showed a downwards-pointing arrow. It meant nothing to Benjamin, and all he could do was to say as much.

'Dear me!' cried Mops. 'Am I going to have to explain *everything*?'

'Probably,' replied Benjamin.

'We are in a place called Lon-denium. It's the biggest and busiest town in the whole Bear Kingdom. So big and so busy, that to help them get from place to place more quickly, the bears dug the Under-Town. That sign shows it's one of the ways in.'

They'd now crept close enough to the cave's entrance for Benjamin to peer inside. The place looked empty. A little hatch in the cave wall was closed and shuttered. Beyond it, all he could see were steps which looked as if they led down into the very depths of the earth.

Then, suddenly, he saw a movement. A short, grey bear was shuffling up the steps. He looked totally miserable.

'Oh, dear,' whispered Mops. 'A ticket-sniffer. I didn't expect to see one of those at this time of sun-come.'

'What's a ticket-sniffer?'

'To travel on the Under-Town you need a ticket. Tickets have different smells depending on where you want to go. Ticket-sniffers check them to make sure bears aren't travelling without paying.'

Benjamin peered cautiously back round the doorway. The grey bear had gone into a cubicle at the top of the stairs and was letting out regular loud yawns. He looked half asleep. Even so, realised Benjamin, one thing was certain. Half asleep or not, there was no way they could get down those steps without the ticket-sniffer spotting them.

THE CIRCLE-LANE

It was Benjamin who had the great idea.

'What happens during this crush-hour?' he asked.

(After seeing the ticket-sniffer, he and Mops had scuttled back to a small cart-park they'd spotted. They were now hiding behind its low wall.)

'Work-bears who work close to their dens go to their jobs on paw or, if they've got a lot of money like bank-bears, they ride in their carts,' said Mops. 'But if they work somewhere else in Lon-denium then they use the Under-Town.'

'All at the same time?'

'It feels like it! My owner only took me on the Under-Town in the crush-hour once. I thought I was going to faint! There were bears jammed in all round us. I dread to think what my nose was pressed against!'

'Humans *can* go on the Under-Town, then?'

'Only if they're with their owners,' said Mops. 'If we try to get past that ticket-sniffer by ourselves, we'll be caught for certain.'

That's when Benjamin had his idea. 'But if we wait till

the crush-hour we won't be on our own, will we? There'll be bears everywhere. Nobody will be able to tell we're not with an owner. They'll all think we belong to some other bear.'

Mops's eyes lit up. 'Benjamin Wildfire, that is *brilliant*!'

So, they waited.

While the orange sun climbed slowly above the horizon, as if it too didn't feel like getting up, grumbling work-bears were heaving themselves up from their soft beds. Breakfasts were being hurriedly eaten. Den doors were creaking open. Goodbye snout-snuffles were being exchanged. The town of Lon-denium was coming alive.

From their hiding place, Benjamin and Mops heard a growing noise of sharp-clawed paws scratching along the road outside. First in ones and twos, then in fives and sixes, until soon the air was filled with the sounds of hurrying paw-steps – not to mention cartwheels creaking, drivers bellowing at walking bears who got in their way and walkers bellowing angrily in reply.

Cautiously, Benjamin stood up and peeped over the wall. Bears were hurrying here, there and everywhere. It shouldn't be difficult to find one who was in so much of a hurry that he or she wouldn't notice two saps trailing along behind them.

'That one!' hissed Mops.

She was pointing at a serious-looking boss-bear (that is, a bear whose job involved telling other bears what to do).

Tied round her portly middle was a large pouch stuffed with papers. Most bears they'd seen had been padding along on all fours. This one had taught herself to walk on her hind legs alone. It meant that she could read one of her papers as she moved. Perfect, thought Benjamin. She wouldn't notice them at all. He took a deep breath. Beside him, Mops gripped the handle of her wheely-box. And then, just as the boss-bear strode by, they stepped quickly out into the hustle and bustle of the crush-hour.

Hearts pounding, they followed the boss-bear the short distance to the Under-Town's gaping entrance. Benjamin and Mops were right behind her. Could they fool the ticket-sniffer?

As the boss-bear quickly wafted her ticket in the general direction of the ticket-sniffer's snout and stomped past, Benjamin and Mops both scurried as close to her side as they dared. With the hordes of bears now flooding past him, the ticket-sniffer simply couldn't sniff everywhere at once. Already looking forward to the end of crush-hour and a nice sit down, the ticket-sniffer gave them no more than a glance. They were through!

Hemmed in on all sides, Benjamin and Mops were carried along in the crush. It was all they could do to stay on their feet and close to the boss-bear – especially when, suddenly, it seemed as if the floor had started moving.

'What's happening?' hissed Benjamin, starting to panic.

'Don't worry,' said Mops, 'It's only a step-move.'

Benjamin tried not to worry, but it wasn't easy with

the floor shifting beneath his feet. 'How does it work?' he asked.

'Don't ask,' said Mops solemnly.

Benjamin didn't press the point. Besides, there were other things to worry about. The step-move was making it hard for Mops to keep her wheely-box under control. She'd already provoked a couple of irritated growls from bears whose paws she'd run over. And the last thing they wanted was to attract any attention, especially as the boss-bear was now some way in front of them. And...*beneath* them!

'We're going down!' whispered Benjamin.

'Really?' sighed Mops, rolling her eyes. 'Well, I never. I wonder if that's why the bears call this the Under-Town?'

'All right,' said Benjamin, feeling stupid. 'How much further is it, then?'

'Nearly there, I think. I remember it being a long way down. And very cold.'

That, Benjamin didn't need to be told. His breath was already freezing on the air and his ears were tingling. By the time the moving staircase reached the end of its journey, Benjamin's toes were tingling too.

Ahead of them, the boss-bear was pushing through a waiting crowd. For one awful moment Benjamin thought they'd lose her completely. Then she stopped at the edge of a big, long trench. Casually, he and Mops slid between her and a scruffy-looking bear who smelled as if he'd recently swallowed rather a lot of squash-grape. Both of them were looking towards a large, round hole in the distance.

Benjamin hissed in Mops's ear. 'What are we waiting for?'

'The next slither-train,' answered Mops, pointing towards the hole. 'It will come out of there.'

Benjamin wasn't sure what a slither-train was, and didn't like to ask. All he hoped was that it would come soon and that it would be warm inside. He was freezing cold, and now he could see why. At the bottom of the big, long trench was a wide ribbon of solid ice which stretched all the way back to the hole. Benjamin knew about ice, of course, from the wintry days when Mrs Haggard had sent him outside and he'd found his water bucket frozen over. Ice was very slippery and horribly cold.

Suddenly the crowd of waiting bears began to stir. An icy crackling noise was growing louder. Thumping sounds soon joined it. Then, from the direction of the hole came a distant roar: 'Hard-pull! Hard-pull!'

The slither-train emerged from the hole with a sudden whoosh. It was the most terrifying sight Benjamin had ever seen. The train was made up of lots of large wagons linked together. Each wagon had polished strips of wood beneath it to help it slither over the ice.

But that wasn't the terrifying part. No, the terrifying part was how the slither-train moved. As it raced closer towards him, Benjamin could see that it was being pulled by a gang of panting, sweating humans.

THE SAP-CATCHER

The train-saps (for that's what the bears called them) were all much older than Benjamin. At least eight or nine summers older, he thought, because they were far bigger and stronger than he was. Each wore a pair of chunky, spiked boots to help them get a foot-grip on the icy floor. They were manacled together in twos. Behind them, crouched at the very front of the first wagon, sat a scowling driver-bear. It was he who now cracked his vicious whip over the youths' bare shoulders and roared, 'Down-slow!' Then, 'Dead-stop!'

By digging their spiked heels into the ice, the gasping youths brought the train to a slithering halt. In front of Benjamin and Mops, the boss-bear was waiting impatiently for others to get out of the wagon nearest to her. She leapt aboard as soon as she was able and quickly found herself a spot in the corner. There, she put the important-looking paper back in her pouch and closed her eyes with all the look of a bear who was settling down for a quick snooze. This suited Benjamin and Mops perfectly. They'd managed to get within touching distance of the boss-bear and she still hadn't noticed they were pretending to be with her.

At the front, the driver's whip cracked again. He let out another fierce roar of 'Hard-pull!' and the poor, sweating youths began to grunt and heave.

Benjamin Wildfire felt desperately sorry for them. He'd thought his life with Mrs Haggard had been bad enough, but compared to pulling a slither-train it was nothing. Suddenly it dawned on him why Mops hadn't wanted to say how the step-move worked. It could only be because somewhere, somehow, deep in the ground beyond the reach of sunlight, that too was being powered by a team of humans.

Slowly, the slither-train began to move. It gathered speed – until, all of a sudden, everything went black.

'What's happening now?' Benjamin hissed anxiously in Mops's ear.

'Don't worry. It'll get light again when we reach the next stop. That's how the Under-Town works. It's just one long tunnel, with places for the slither-train to stop and let bears on and off.'

'Where does it end?' asked Benjamin.

'It doesn't,' said Mops. 'It just goes round in a circle.'

'You mean if we stay on here long enough we'll get back to where we started!'

'Exactly,' said Mops calmly. 'But nobody does. They only do that when they finish work and it's time for them to go home again. Then they have the sun-go crush-hour.' She motioned to the boss-bear, still snoozing nearby. 'Believe me, she'll be getting off soon.'

But the boss-bear didn't get off soon. At the next stop she didn't even flick open her eyes. Nor at the next stop. At the stop after that she glanced quickly out, but then closed her eyes again.

Benjamin Wildfire was getting worried. The wagon they were in was now far less crowded. Eyes were beginning to turn their way. Benjamin inched as close to the dozing boss-bear as he dared.

Outside, the drive-bear was cracking her whip and shouting 'Dead-stop!' yet again. The slither-train began to slow. And, this time, the boss-bear did take notice. She yawned. She stretched. She adjusted the pouch of papers around her middle. Then, as the slither-train came to a halt, she moved towards the wagon door.

'Go!' hissed Benjamin.

Mops moved quickly after the boss-bear, the rumbling of her wheely-box drowned out by the gasping and panting of the exhausted train-saps. Benjamin couldn't bring himself to look at them. Hunching his bag of supplies over his shoulder, he hurried close to Mops's side. All he wanted to think about was following the boss-bear away from this horror, then quickly finding a new hiding place where they could decide what to do next.

In front of them, the boss-bear was getting her ticket out to be sniffed. And if Benjamin Wildfire hadn't been thinking so hard about what it was going to be like outside, he might have noticed that the ticket-sniffer at this stop was very different to the one they'd seen earlier. This one was a young, bright-eyed bear with protruding ears who'd only been ticket-sniffing for twenty sun-comes. As a result, he was still *very* keen and *very* alert.

He sniffed the boss-bear's ticket thoroughly, then waved her through with a toothy smile. But when Benjamin and Mops tried to scurry through as well, the young sniffer's attitude changed completely.

'Sap-tickets!' he demanded, stepping abruptly in front of the boss-bear and pointing at Benjamin and Mops.

The boss-bear swung round. She glared down at Benjamin and Mops. Her snout wrinkled in disgust. 'Not-them me-with!'

'Then who-with?' demanded the young ticket-sniffer.

Behind them, a small queue of work-bears had built up. They'd all been grumbling about the unexpected delay, but as the ticket-sniffer spoke they fell silent. Furry heads shook.

'Must-be somebody-with,' snapped the ticket-sniffer. 'Rules so-say.'

'Thinks-me them me-with,' growled a cold voice from somewhere in the background.

Benjamin shuddered. Stalking upright towards them was a huge bear with piercing eyes and the longest, sharpest claws he'd ever seen. In those long, sharp claws the bear was holding a scratch-pad. Mrs Haggard had had one a bit like it. Dipping a claw into a dark liquid, she'd scratch notes on its sheets of parchment about things she wanted to remember. But her pad had been quite small. This bear's was far bigger and more impressive-looking. For a start, it had a picture of a royal crown on the back.

Scurrying beside the great bear were two smaller bears (they could hardly have been bigger). Each was unravelling a coil of thick rope from around their waist.

'Run, Mops!' yelled Benjamin.

It was no use. Before they'd even started to move, the great bear had grabbed Benjamin with one powerful paw and the keen ticket-sniffer had taken hold of Mops. In no time at all the pair of them were being tied up.

This done, the bear with piercing eyes began to use his scratch-pad. Using a sharp claw, he ticked here and jotted there, speaking crisply to the young ticket-sniffer as he did so.

'By command-royal, take-me now saps-these!'

'Y-yes, Sir.'

'Are-them owners-abandoned. Correct?'

'If say-you-so, Sir,' stammered the ticket-sniffer.

'Me-do. Say-me also are-them danger-public.'

'Are-them?'

'Yes! And you witness-mine!' Holding the pad beneath the ticket-sniffer's snout, the bear with piercing eyes snapped, 'Here-sign!'

The young ticket-sniffer scratched a cross at the bottom of the completed form, then quickly bowed and shrank back.

'Now me-with come-they. Understand?'

The ticket-sniffer nodded rapidly.

Benjamin didn't know what was happening, but he knew it wasn't good. The huge bear was making it up. He and Mops hadn't been abandoned exactly. Neither had they been causing the slightest danger.

'I don't want to go with him!' yelled Benjamin. 'Neither does Mops!'

'Definitely not!' screeched Mops. 'I'd much rather go back home if you don't mind. I can show you the way. I'm very well educated!'

Her voice had risen to a loud shrill as she said these final words because the giant bear had turned his piercing eyes on her. What was more, he'd now handed his scratch-pad to one of his helpers and was stalking slowly towards her.

'Don't you dare touch her!' shouted Benjamin.

'He's right!' screamed Mops. 'Don't you dare touch me!'

Of course, to the bear with piercing eyes and sharp claws, all this noise meant nothing. He couldn't understand a word they were shouting. But let's be clear about this: it wouldn't have made a scrap of difference if he *had*. He would still have done what he did – which was to dip the longest and sharpest of the claws on his right forepaw into a small pot of liquid that his helper had produced, and then jab that claw sharply into the top part of Mops's pale arm.

He did exactly the same to the struggling Benjamin. It was the most curious sensation. Benjamin hardly had time to yelp with pain before he began to feel very, very tired. Beside him he was vaguely aware of Mops sinking to the floor with a little sigh. Then, try as he might to prevent it, Benjamin felt his own eyes beginning to close.

The second to last thing that Benjamin heard was the bear with piercing eyes and sharp claws telling the ticket-sniffer, 'Done-you-well.'

The last thing was the proud ticket-sniffer's reply. 'You-thank, Inspector Sap-Catcher!'

THE HOWLING-TOWER

Benjamin Wildfire's eyes felt as heavy as Mrs Haggard's wicked chain. With an effort he forced them open. His head felt fuzzy, as if he'd only just woken from an uncomfortable night in his spot by the back door. But that fuzziness had always cleared the instant the scraggy old bear had stomped out of her sleeping-chamber and kicked him in the ribs. *This* fuzziness wouldn't go away, even though Benjamin's ribs were being bounced up and down in much the same manner.

He was lying on wooden boards. Bouncing wooden boards. Through the fuzziness Benjamin worked out that he'd been dumped in a cart — a cart that was taking him along a rough track to somewhere. Taking *them* to somewhere. A pink-dressed but unmoving figure, squashed up against him, told Benjamin that Mops was in the cart too.

They weren't alone. The cart was full. Benjamin couldn't push out a hand or a foot without it bumping into a curled-up body. Outside, dusk was falling. The huge bear and his helpers must have been out capturing stray humans since just after sun-come. Perhaps that was why he'd started to wake up, because he and Mops had been put to sleep first, having been caught so early in the day.

He found it hard not to think about how little time they'd been free. And he found it even harder not to think about the awful sight of those train-saps, because from the puffing and groaning he could hear it was clear that a similar team of humans was pulling the cart he was in.

They bumped on. As it grew darker, they began to pass by lighted torch-posts. Each time they did so, Benjamin would glimpse the outlines of the bent-backed cart-pullers – and, ahead of them, the terrifying silhouette of the sharp-clawed Sap-Catcher.

Where was he taking them? The answer to that question soon began to loom out of the darkness. Pin-pricks of light were the first clue – flickering lights, which moved from side to side low in the purple sky. Cart-bump by cart-bump they grew larger, until Benjamin fuzzily realised that these lights were also torches of flame. They were lined up along the top of a massive white wall. And the reason they were moving to and fro was that each was being held in the rough paw of a guard-bear on sentry duty.

The cart slowed and stopped. Benjamin lifted himself warily up on to his elbows for a fuzzy look. Set into the centre of the thick white wall he saw an imposing wooden gate, with gigantic hinges and iron studs as big as his own head.

The sharp-clawed bear strode forward and thumped fiercely on the gate. Benjamin thought the walls trembled, but it could have been the fuzziness in his head.

'Up-open!' bellowed the bear.

A guard-bear looked down from the top of the wall. 'Who there-goes?'

'Inspector Dictatum!'

'Inspec—' The torch at the top of the wall began to shake violently. 'Y-yes, Sir. Away-straight, Sir!'

Clanking and winding noises began. Slowly, the gate growled open. The cart gave a jolt, causing Benjamin to fall back. It was just as well. For no sooner had the cart trundled through the gate into a large, cobble-stoned courtyard than it stopped again and Inspector Dictatum was issuing yet more orders.

'Sap-things to store-cave!' he barked. Then, 'Saps to Doctor Calcupod for number-marking!'

Benjamin shut his eyes tight and let everything else flop. Something told him it would be a good idea to pretend that he was still knocked out.

So he felt, rather than saw, his bag taken from him. He heard Mops's spangly-wheeled wheely-box being trundled away. Then he both felt and heard himself being lifted from the cart and carried along an echoing corridor by a pair of puffing guard-bears.

When they stopped, a soft growl – almost a purr – said,

'Here-him-bring.' Doctor Calcupod, it had to be.

Benjamin felt himself being laid on something flat and wooden. A table, of sorts. From nearby came different sounds: of scratching quills and rustling parchment, like the sounds Mrs Haggard made when she wrote out the lists of new lotions and potions she wanted to try.

The soft voice spoke again. 'Sap-number one four three seven two...'

From close by a claw scratched on parchment, then paused until the same voice continued, '...Benjamin Wildfire.'

How in Bear Kingdom did she know his name? wondered Benjamin – but only until a set of claws closed around his throat and gently undid his name collar. *That* was how.

'Wildfire?' he heard Doctor Calcupod hum. 'A name-uncommon. But...catch-we not another Wildfire many moons-ago, Inspector Dictatum?'

'No!'

'Sure-you? Memory-mine usually-is very name-good.'

'No! Never!'

'Derek Wildfire? Dominic Wildfire? Duncan Wildfire? Could-me easily records-check...'

'No!' roared the Inspector again. 'Not-have any Wildfires here-been since arrive-me! Now on-get with number-marking!'

50

At that point Benjamin's eyes were still firmly shut. But one of the names Doctor Calcupod had mentioned was slowly penetrating the fuzziness in his head. Duncan Wildfire? The name of his very own father! Could it possibly be that he'd been brought here? The thought made Benjamin's heart leap. More than that – it made him open his eyes.

From left to right, he saw four bears.

First, a help-bear, holding open a bulky, black-bound scratch-pad.

Second, another help-bear, an ink-stained claw showing that it had been he who'd just scratched down Benjamin's name and sap-number.

Next a short, well-groomed she-bear with a thin pointed snout. It could only be Doctor Calcupod. Having dropped Benjamin's name-collar into a big sack, she was now dipping a needle-sharp claw into a bowl of green liquid.

Finally, Benjamin spied the towering figure of Inspector Dictatum. His eyes were darting everywhere, inspecting everything and missing nothing...

'Sap-that awake-is!' he roared.

And so it was that Benjamin had two final memories of that small room. One, the sensation of his left shirtsleeve being rolled up by Doctor Calcupod. The other, of a piercing pain in his right arm as Inspector Dictatum put him to sleep once more.

NUMBER TWELVE...
AND SPIKE

When Benjamin woke again, it was to sounds of squishing and slurping. A few drops of water spattered briefly across his face, then stopped. A bucket clanked.

Benjamin groaned. His whole body ached from being bounced in the Sap-Catcher's cart. Both his arms were throbbing too.

He turned his head and warily opened his eyes. No Doctor Calcupod. No help-bears. No Inspector Dictatum. He was somewhere different. He was in a room with stripes on the wall. He stretched out a hand. No, he wasn't. He was in a room with stripes *for* one of the four walls. They were cold and hard and very real. They were bars. Benjamin was in a cage. He groaned again.

'Hooray,' said a girl's voice, 'awake at last!'

'Mops!'

She was sitting on the floor beside him, leaning against one of the solid walls. Her pretty hair was bedraggled, her fluffy pink dress torn.

'You look a mess,' said Benjamin, sitting up slowly.

'Who wouldn't!' cried Mops indignantly. 'I defy any girl to sparkle after spending a night cooped up in a place like this. There's hardly enough room to swing a comb!'

It was true. The cage was so narrow that it couldn't have measured more than three steps from one wall to the other. Neither was it deep. From the bars to the end would be six steps at most, he thought. The only consolation was that the cage was at least high enough for him to stand up with room to spare. This Benjamin was about to do, until Mops sat him down again.

'Why don't we save exploring our new home for later?' she said. 'It will give us *so* much to look forward to – I don't think!'

Apart from themselves the cage held little else. A bowl of water sat in one corner. A second (empty) bowl was chained to the end wall. The only other thing in the cage was a heap of grubby straw at the far end.

Mops waved a furious arm. 'Just look at the state of this floor. It can't have been cleaned for *moons*!'

'Not my job, cages,' said a voice. 'I'm corridors, not cages. You want a clean cage, do it yourself.'

Benjamin gasped. The voice belonged to a booted figure wearing bright orange overalls and a bright orange cap. The figure was moving along a corridor on the other side of the bars. It was carrying a bucket and a soggy brush – the brush that must have been squishing and slurping and spattering Benjamin with water as he woke up. None of these things were gasp-worthy, however. What had made Benjamin gasp was the fact that the figure wasn't that of a bear, but of a man. Quite an ancient man, about forty summers he guessed, but a human for all that. What's more, he was free.

'Who are you?' asked Benjamin. 'Why aren't you locked up?'

'Does it matter?' cried Mops. 'Just get in here with that brush. Do your duty!'

'I told you,' replied the brush-holder, 'I'm corridors, not cages. I haven't been trained for cages.'

Mops snorted in disgust, momentarily lost for words. This gave Benjamin the chance to ask his questions again. 'Who are you? Why aren't you locked up?'

This time the man answered. 'I'm not locked up because I'm a trusty-sap,' he said loftily. 'Trained and trusted, which means I don't have to be locked up. And as to who I am — my name is Twelve.'

'Twelve?' cried Mops, finding her voice again. 'That's not a name, that's a number!'

'It's all I've got.'

'But you must have had a proper name once,' said Benjamin, who simply couldn't imagine forgetting his name, or those of Alicia his mother and Duncan his father. His memories of their faces might grow hazier, but nothing would make him break his vow to keep their names burning in his heart.

The trusty-sap shook his head. 'Humans don't have names, not in 'ere. First thing they does, that is. They takes away your name and gives you a number.'

'Bah!' scoffed Mops. 'I don't believe that for a moment.'

'No? So where's your name-collars, then?'

Benjamin's hand flew to his throat, just as Mops's did to hers. Their name-collars had gone.

'See?' said Twelve.

A memory drifted fuzzily back into Benjamin's mind. Doctor Calcupod, dropping his collar into a sack and reaching for something. A bowl of green liquid...

Benjamin wrenched up his left sleeve. The pain in his right arm was down to Inspector Dictatum's sleeping jab. Now he saw why his other arm was hurting too. High up, just above the elbow, was a number.

'One Four Three Seven Two,' read Twelve. 'Big!'

'One Four Three Seven Three,' murmured Mops. She had peeled back her pink sleeve and was staring, moist-eyed, at the number scratched into the skin of her own arm. 'The disgrace of it: a Snubnose turned into a number...'

Benjamin would have liked to learn more about Mops's family history but now was not the time to ask.

'A number's not so bad when you get used to it,' said Twelve.

'I will never get used to it!' snapped Mops. 'Especially in *green*!'

'And I'll never forget my name!' shouted Benjamin. 'Benjamin Wildfire! Benjamin Wildfire! Benjamin Wildfire——'

His chanting was interrupted by the loud clattering of a bucket. Number Twelve had dropped it and was staring at him. 'Wildfire, did you say?'

'Yes,' nodded Benjamin.

His heart fluttered. Another fuzzy memory surfaced, this time of Doctor Calcupod arguing with Inspector Dictatum about the arrival of another sap named Wildfire in moons gone by.

'My father's name was – is – Duncan Wildfire. My mother's name is Alicia. Why, have you heard of them? Have they been in here? Tell me!'

Twelve shook his head vigorously. His ruddy face, which for a moment had gone quite pale – or so it seemed to Benjamin – was back to normal.

'Duncan Wildfire? Alicia Wildfire? No. No, no, no, no no. Never heard of them.'

'Are you sure?'

'Qu-quite sure,' stammered Twelve unconvincingly. 'I can't remember having any Wildfires in this place.'

'And what, precisely, *is* this place?' demandedMops, who'd been tearfully fingering the green number on her arm.

Twelve looked relieved at the change of subject of human names. Picking up the bucket he'd just dropped he turned it over and sat down.

'This place,' he said slowly, 'is the Howling-Tower. That's not its proper name, but it's what the bears all call it.'

Mops stomped up to the bars of the cage and shook them with both hands. 'Will you please stop talking in riddles! What is its proper name, then? What are we doing here? And most important of all,' she screeched, 'when do we get out?'

Twelve seemed unsure about what to do next. He looked both ways along the corridor. He seemed to spend an awfully long time looking thoughtfully at Benjamin Wildfire. Then, slowly, he started again.

'This place is an official Bear Kingdom department. It's proper name is *Outpost-For Sap-Training, Education, Deployment*. But, as I say, the bears call it the Howling-Tower.'

'I can't say I blame them,' sniffed Mops. 'What a mouthful!'

'But what does it mean?' asked Benjamin. 'Does it explain what goes on here?'

'Well...yes,' said Twelve hesitantly. 'It means it's a place where humans of all ages are trained and educated and—'

'Deployed,' said Mops. 'What does that mean?'

'Given jobs. Like corridor cleaning. That's what happened to me all those moons ago. Except that – well, things have changed since Inspector Dictatum arrived. He goes in for trading rather than

57

training. More profitable. So his rule is that any humans brought in are only given five sun-comes, six at most, for their owners to come and buy them back.'

'Well for goodness' sake, why didn't you say so?' cried Mops. 'That's not so bad. My owner must have been positively grief-stricken when she found out I'd gone. They only have to contact her at the address on the back of my name-collar and she'll be here in a trice.'

Number Twelve's eyebrows rose. 'Possibly,' was all he said.

Benjamin was thinking ahead. It was all right for Mops, but the prospect of Mrs Haggard turning up and taking him back wasn't at all nice – especially if she fulfilled her parting threat about making him wish he'd been never-born.

'What if our owners don't come?' he asked.

'Trading, remember? You'll be taken to Fleeceham Market for another five days. Any bear who likes the look of you can buy you—'

'If they can afford me,' interrupted Mops. 'We Snubnoses are worth a fortune. We've got breeding. An awfully fine family background...'

But Number Twelve was no longer listening. From somewhere outside a klaxon had begun to wail. Leaping to his feet, the trusty-sap snatched up his bucket and brush before scurrying away along the corridor.

'Well!' said Mops, hands on hips. 'How rude!'

Benjamin was deep in thought. It sounded as if he'd

either be going back to Mrs Haggard (if she came for him) or ending up with an owner who might be even worse. Before yesterday he wouldn't have thought that possible, but after seeing those suffering train-saps and cart-saps...

'Mops,' he said urgently, 'we've got to find a way out of here.'

'No chance, matey,' said a voice from the end of the cage.

Startled, Benjamin and Mops both looked that way. The pile of grubby straw was moving. A crop-haired head had begun to appear. It was followed by a freckled nose, then by a mouth with two front teeth missing, then by a neck in serious need of a good wash.

'Good grief!' said Mops, quite loudly.

Benjamin was more polite, especially as the emerging figure had proved to be a boy of about the same age as himself. 'Hello,' he said. 'Who are you? And why *shouldn't* we find a way out of here?'

'The name's Spike Brownberry...' replied the grubby boy.

He paused. The klaxon had finished wailing. Spike pointed. Slowly, and accompanied by the sound of clanking chains, a small, square section of the cage's solid end wall began to move jerkily upwards. Only then did Spike add: '...And as for why you've got no chance of finding a way out of here – you're about to see that for yourself, matey.'

THE RUNAROUND-YARD

The proper name for the movable section at the end of their cage was an Out-Way. But throughout the Howling-Tower they were known as sap-flaps because, once they'd been fully winched up, they provided just enough room for an average-sized sap to crawl through. Following Spike's lead, Benjamin and Mops did just that.

'The runaround-yard,' announced Spike, with a sweep of his arm. 'Run, jump and play, if you feel like it. I don't.'

Benjamin knew what he meant. Calling it the runaround-yard was cruel, for you only ran around when you were happy. Here, nobody was. The humans slowly emerging from beneath the row of sap-flaps (Benjamin could see what he'd already suspected, that their cage was but one in a whole block of them) looked as frightened and miserable as he felt. That wasn't the only thing they had in common. They were also all young. The older captives – Benjamin was sure there must be some, such as the cart-pullers – were presumably kept in other blocks.

Apart from being horribly named, the runaround-yard was also horrible to look at. It made Mrs Haggard's garden look lush and well kept. The ground was threadbare and dry, with just an odd tuft of hardy grass sticking up. Only a patch of scruffy bushes in one corner looked as though they might be worth exploring. At least, they did until Spike called over his shoulder: 'Them bushes are where everybody does their business.'

Spike was heading towards the shade of a lonely tree, growing beside the runaround-yard fence. Benjamin followed him to see if it, at least, was worth climbing. It wasn't. All he'd get was a better view of the fence – and he could see it quite well enough from the ground, unfortunately.

Unlike Mrs Haggard's fence, this fence was made from strong, unbreakable wire. More wire ran along the top of the fence; a different sort though, all coiled and spiky and vicious. Benjamin saw at once that climbing over this fence would be impossible.

Spike had seated himself on a round rock – by the look of it, the only rock in the whole runaround-yard. Benjamin squatted miserably down beside him.

'How long have you been here, then?' he asked Spike.

'Not much longer than you. They brought me here yesterday sun-high.'

'Had you run away like us?'

Spike shook his head. 'Dumped, weren't I?'

'Dumped? Why?'

'Usual story. You're a bear-cub's present. For a while everything's fine, all oohs and aahs and plenty of treats. You're the number one attraction. Then you get bigger, do your business in the wrong place, sick up a feed or two and, wallop – they've had enough. Into the cart, down to the river and in you go. By the time I'd swum to the bank they'd gone.'

'Lucky you could swim,' said Benjamin.

'Not really,' said Spike. 'I got nabbed as soon I reached the bank. I've only just dried out. I hate water.'

'And washing, judging by the state of your hands!' said Mops, dusting the ground before sitting down too.

Spike sniffed and snorted at the same time (not easy). 'I'm a Brownberry. Brownberrys are cleaner than they look.' He turned to Benjamin. 'Squawker your friend, is she?'

'Squawker?' squawked Mops. 'How dare you! I'll have you know my name is Millicent Ophelia Patience Snubnose.'

'Mops to her friends,' smiled Benjamin.

Mops pointed an imperious finger at Spike. 'But you may call me Miss Snubnose.'

'I'll call you more than that if you don't watch it,' growled Spike. 'I heard what you said to Twelve. "I've got breeding!" Hah, try that on *them*!'

As he said this, Spike jerked a thumb towards a couple

of bulky guard-bears stationed just beyond the fence. Bristling with menace, they looked as if nothing would give them greater pleasure than stopping any sap who was foolish enough to make an escape bid.

'Now I see what you mean about the chances of getting away,' Benjamin said.

Spike leaned his back against the trunk of the tree, nodding miserably. 'Yep,' he sighed, 'I've heard there's only one way out of here—'

'To be sold at the market!' interrupted Mops with a wail. 'Oh, why didn't I stay where I was comfortable? Why did I listen to your silly stories, Benjamin Wildfire?'

'What story's that, then?' asked Spike.

Benjamin felt embarrassed. 'A story my parents told me when I was little. About a wonderful place called Hide-Park where humans are free to do what they like.'

'Gah!' spat Spike. 'That old sap-tale. Everybody knows Hide-Park's just a place invented by humans to give themselves something to dream about.'

Benjamin didn't argue. They could say what they liked. He believed in Hide-Park and always would. They'd believe it too, when he found it. Because somehow he *was* going to find it.

'As I was saying,' said Spike, back to being miserable, 'what I've heard is there's only one way out of here.' He pointed at Mops. 'And I don't mean the market either...I mean the Mincer.'

'The what?' gasped Benjamin.

'The Mincer. When the bears can't use a sap any more they chuck 'em in and they get…minced.'

A mincer? Like the one Mrs Haggard had used to shred leaves and roots in an attempt to make her own lotions and potions (none of which worked any better than those she bought) – but large enough to take a human instead of a leaf or a root? Surely not!

'And you call *my* story a sap-tale!' Benjamin laughed.

'Please yerself,' said Spike. 'We'll all find out the truth about the Mincer soon enough.'

Mops put her hands over her ears. 'Stop! I forbid you to utter that horrid word in my presence again!'

'What – Mincer?'

'Waaahhh!!' screeched Mops.

Spike shrugged. 'All right, Squawker. Anyway, from what I've heard you don't feel a thing. One quick wallop on the head and it's all over. Course, no boy or girl's ever come back to say otherwise. By then they're already on their way to some bear's dinner table.'

'Dinner?' said Benjamin. He didn't want to continue this conversation any more than Mops, but it had become horribly fascinating. 'You don't mean bears *eat* humans?'

'Not all of 'em, no. Lots of bears stick to vegetables and fruits. But plenty do. Oh, yes. We could come out of the Mincer as a string of sap-sages.'

'They can't do that to me!' wailed Mops. 'I'm too pretty to be turned into a sap-sage!'

'Oh, you won't just be turned into sap-sages,' said Spike with the certain air of one who knew about these things. 'Some of your bits could end up being roasted. Or shovelled into a tasty pie. Nothing goes to waste, I've heard.'

'Stop it, stop it!'

Benjamin had heard enough, too. What with the fence and the patrolling guard-bears squashing any hope of escape, and now Spike's terrible tales of ending up in the Mincer (even if he didn't believe a word of them), Benjamin had never felt unhappier. As the klaxon sounded to signal the end of runaround time, he told himself that things could only get better.

He was wrong.

A SAP'S LIFE

The moment they were back in their cage, chains rattled and the heavy sap-flaps slammed shut with an echo that rang the length and breadth of the cage-block. Those flaps wouldn't open again until just before sun-go…not fully, anyway.

They would open slightly, though. Twice. Once before the sun reached its highest and once when it had begun to sink down towards the forbidding white walls with their patrolling bear-sentries. On both occasions the sap-flaps would clank up for a short distance and stop. Paws would reach in for the heavy, square bowl chained to the wall. It would vanish, only to clatter back under the sap-flap moments later.

The bowl would have been filled with food – although that wasn't the word Mops used when their first meal arrived.

'That is disgusting!' she cried. 'Eat that? I'd rather starve!'

Spike wasn't so fussy and neither was Benjamin. Compared to some of the scraps Mrs Haggard had given him, the mixture in the bowl didn't look too bad. The berries and acorns seemed almost fresh. So did the roots and leaves. It was the unidentifiable chunks of gristly, meaty stuff that looked the nastiest. But eating was better than starving – a conclusion that Mops also came to after a short while. Closing her eyes and holding her nose she began to pluck bits from the bowl, trying to swallow them without catching any of the taste.

Afterwards they settled down, wondering which of them in the cage-block would be the first to have their owner turn up and buy them back. Sure enough, it wasn't too long before they saw bear-shaped shadows fall across the square windows in the corridor wall. The shouting began even before the visitors had set a paw inside the cage-block.

'Here I am!' cried a tearful girl. 'Take me home!'

'Get me out of here!' yelled a desperate boy.

Mops wasted no time in adding her voice to the clamour. 'Don't take any notice of them! I'm prettier! I'm better den-trained! I'm everything you want in one lovable bundle...'

But they all fell silent as, one by one, they realised that the visitor wasn't that sort of visitor at all. It was Doctor Calcupod. She began to pad slowly along the corridor, her thin snout twitching as she stopped at each cage in turn. Behind her trailed the same two help-bears.

'One Four Three Seven One...' said Doctor Calcupod, looking at Spike. 'Big-strong.'

The first help-bear (named Lectern, in case you were wondering) was holding a scarlet-coloured scratch-pad this time, one slightly smaller and not quite so worn as the huge black sap-numbering scratch-pad that Benjamin had seen the previous night. Now, as Docter Calcupod spoke, Lectern held the pad steady for the second help-bear (named Clericus) to scratch a note with the tip of his inky writing claw. By the time he'd finished, Doctor Calcupod had already moved on and was studying Benjamin Wildfire very closely indeed.

'One Four Three Seven Two...' she purred. 'Ahh, the hair-red. Could-me him-use many-ways.' Clericus made a note of the decision.

Mops was ready and waiting. 'Are you responsible for this number on my arm?' she screeched as Doctor Calcupod looked in at her. 'Do you know the first thing about colour co-ordination? Green is simply not *me*!'

Doctor Calcupod ignored the yapping (she couldn't understand a word of it, of course). 'One four three seven three...noise-loud.'

'What was that all about?' said Benjamin once they'd gone.

'Who knows,' said Spike glumly, 'but if she was looking for saps to turn into sap-sages she can keep on saying no to me for as long as she likes.'

They settled down again, waiting...and waiting...and waiting...until, long after the sun had started to drift down in the sky like an orange bubble, Twelve arrived.

'Still here?' he said to everybody as he sloshed along the corridor with his bucket and brush. 'Ah well, maybe tomorrow.'

'But we haven't seen a single owner,' said Benjamin. 'Not one.'

'No?' said Twelve, moving quickly past.

Mops shook her curls indignantly. 'No. Not even mine. I am completely and utterly stunned. To know I'm here and not come for me? I can't believe it!'

'You will,' said Twelve mysteriously. Saying no more, he hurried away.

The klaxon sounded not long after. Up rattled the sap-flaps to allow the food bowls to be pushed in for their second and final meal of the day. A short gap followed to let the food go down. Then, with a clattering and clanking of chains, the sap-flaps were winched slowly up to their full height. Out they crawled to stretch their stiff legs.

By that time sun-go was near. The orange ball had sunk behind the Howling-Tower's white walls, making the beaten earth of the runaround-yard look much darker. The branches of the tree now cast deep shadows. The wire fence looked even higher, and its vicious barbed top extra-forbidding.

Benjamin, Mops and Spike walked slowly round and round the yard, just inside the fence. By the time they'd done a few laps sun-go was almost complete. Beyond the white walls of the Howling-Tower just a blood-red glow hung in the sky.

'Time to go in!' said Spike suddenly.

'Why? How do you know?' asked Benjamin.

'Just do it!' Spike shouted, then started racing for their sap-flap.

Mops shrugged. 'Strange boy. Almost as strange as he is grubby.'

Benjamin wasn't so sure. Many of the other boys and girls in the runaround-yard were scrambling urgently back into their cages too. And Spike had clearly been right about one thing. The klaxon had now begun to wail, a special up-and-down wail this time which they would come to realise signalled the end of the Howling-Tower day. The guard-bears outside the fence, who until then had been lounging around looking bored, were pointing and shouting, 'In-get!'

Reluctantly, they dawdled towards their sap-flap, wanting to breathe every last drop of fresh air that they could. Only when they saw two powerful guard-bears appear, marching in step towards the far end of the cage-block, did Benjamin suggest that it might be a good idea not to linger any longer.

They slid beneath the sap-flap. Almost at once there came the fierce rattle of unwinding chains and down rumbled the sap-flap to hit the floor of the cage with a solid, no-way-out clunk.

Spike had vanished. Well, not vanished exactly, for

they could see where he was. He'd buried himself beneath his pile of straw. It was quivering.

'Spike, are you all right?' asked Benjamin. No answer. 'Spike!' He poked the quivering pile with his finger. 'I said are you all right?'

Spike's grubby, freckled face appeared for just an instant – but that was enough for Benjamin to see that his eyes were filled with terror.

'He'll be coming soon!' was all he cried before jamming his fingers in his ears and diving back into his straw pile.

'Who?' was all Benjamin had time to say.

Then both he and Mops were plugging their ears and diving beneath the straw pile as they tried to stop themselves being deafened by the most terrifying noise they'd ever heard in their young lives.

INSPECTOR DICTATUM

The terrifying noise was that of Inspector Dictatum on his rounds, no less terrifying for the fact that it began with a quiet *chuff-puff*.

Inspector Dictatum began every round full of fierce thoughts about what he would do if any sap decided to cause him trouble. Troublesome saps made him agitated and when bears are agitated *chuff-puff* is the sound they make.

The great bear moved menacingly towards the first cage-block on his route – the block, it just so happened, in which Benjamin, Mops and Spike were cowering. Approaching it, his *chuff-puff* changed to a *hiss-growl*; for that is the sound bears make when they are uneasy or angry (or both).

Inspector Dictatum was always uneasy *and* angry. His authority and reputation depended on one thing above any other: never letting a sap escape from his clutches. Every night the mere thought of a sap trying to escape made him uneasy. And, as for the thought of such a thing actually happening – that made him *so* angry!

Finally, the *hiss-growl* grew into Inspector Dictatum's roar: a roar which rumbled up from deep down inside him before bursting forth like an erupting volcano.

Those who don't know much about bears think they roar all the time. But in truth, bears only roar when they are hurt.

So what hurt Inspector Dictatum enough, night after night, to cause him to roar as he did? A memory. A hurtful, painful memory of the one and only time a sap had escaped from the Howling-Tower. And nothing hurt him more than recalling that accursed sap's name.

Duncan Wildfire.

From then on, Inspector Dictatum had taken matters into his own paws. Now, every night, after he'd returned to the Howling-Tower from his sap-catching expeditions, the guard-bears were packed off to their beds. They didn't like it, of course, hated it in fact, for it meant far less pay. But Inspector Dictatum refused to budge. He would control and terrify the saps in the Howling-Tower without help. Alone and unaided he would make certain that never again would he be embarrassed by the likes of Duncan Wildfire.

Inspector Dictatum couldn't forget that name, even though he'd hoped that every other bear in the Howling-Tower had. Doctor Calcupod's questioning the previous night had come as a nasty surprise. And it seemed that he'd captured another Wildfire. A relative? wondered Inspector Dictatum.

Could the new Wildfire possibly be related to the long-escaped Duncan Wildfire? His son, even? Probably not – but, just in case, wouldn't it be a good idea to do his worst to this Benjamin Wildfire sap?

Inspector Dictatum's yellow teeth glinted in the moonlight. Of course it would. This angry thought made Inspector Dictatum roar as he'd never roared before.

Roooooaaaaaaaaaaaaaarrrrrr!

BENJAMIN'S CALCULATION

It was during his fifth night in the Howling-Tower that Benjamin Wildfire made an interesting discovery.

He was unable to sleep – again. This was no different to the previous four nights, of course. Inspector Dictatum's roaring saw to that. But on this night, Benjamin had another thing to worry about.

'This is yer fifth sun-come,' Twelve had said to them during his corridor-cleaning session. 'It'll be the sap market for you three, tomorrow.'

Benjamin could hear Spike's steady breathing. Somehow, he'd managed to fall asleep. But the fearful cries and whimpers coming from other cages in the block showed that Spike was one of the few who had. A restless turning from Mops's part of the cage told Benjamin that she wasn't asleep either.

'Do you think any of us will be sold?' he whispered. 'Spike, maybe?'

'Who in Bear Kingdom would want to buy that scruff-bag!' hissed Mops in the darkness.

They sank back into silence, both of them worrying about what sun-come would bring. Outside,

Inspector Dictatum's almost non-stop racket continued.

Inspector Dictatum, you see, didn't only chuff, puff, hiss, growl and roar when he *began* his inspections. He kept his terrifying noises going throughout the night. They would be shatteringly loud when he was just outside their cage-block. Then the noises would sink lower and softer as he stomped on to inspect other cage-blocks. For a short period, when he was out of range, there would be the most beautiful silence. Then, just as everybody was dropping off to sleep, back he would come, causing cries of fear all along the corridor as his chuffs, puffs, hisses, growls and roars grew to their shattering peak and Inspector Dictatum was right outside their cage-block again.

That, in a way, was what led Benjamin to make his discovery. 'How can Spike sleep through all that?' he whispered.

'Try counting bear-cubs,' mumbled Mops. 'Little, fluffy, cuddly ones. That's what I'm doing...'

'Does it work?' asked Benjamin.

But Mops didn't reply. She'd fallen asleep. So Benjamin began counting bear-cubs. He started when Inspector's Dictatum's roar was at its loudest.

'One, two, three...'

He carried on counting as the noise fell, hoping he'd be asleep by the time it peaked again. But he wasn't. He'd got as far as, 'Two thousand two hundred and eleven, two thousand two hundred and twelve, two thousand two hundred and thirteen…' when Inspector Dictatum's roar from right outside the runaround-yard made Benjamin's cage bars rattle.

He started again. Still sleep wouldn't come. He'd reached, 'two thousand two hundred and twelve…' again when the loudest roar told Benjamin that Inspector Dictatum had arrived back outside once more.

Benjamin began counting for a third time. This time, though, he desperately didn't want to fall asleep. He very much wanted to stay awake.

'One, two, three …' he counted, on and on, up and up as the Inspector's fearsome noises faded and grew until, as the dreadful bear drew up outside the runaround-yard once more, Benjamin found that yet again he'd got as far as, 'two thousand two hundred and twelve…'

It could mean only one thing. Whatever route Inspector Dictatum was following around the mysterious caverns and gloomy cage-blocks of the Howling-Tower, it was the same route every single time. Which meant, realised Benjamin, that any boy (or girl) who could get out of his (or her) cage just as Inspector Dictatum was moving away could be sure of a gap of two thousand two hundred and twelve counts before he came back again.

Interesting.

FLEECEHAM MARKET

Benjamin was woken at the crack of sun-come.

'Up-get!'

He felt as if he'd only just dropped off to sleep – which was exactly as he should have expected to feel, for after all his painstaking counting Benjamin *had* only just fallen asleep. The interesting discovery he'd made came briefly to mind, only to vanish immediately as a heavy paw dug sharply into his ribs.

'Up-get!'

Blearily, Benjamin struggled to his feet. Out in the corridor, Spike and Mops were receiving much the same treatment from another guard-bear.

'But I haven't washed yet!' Mops was objecting. 'I must look a complete mess!'

Naturally, the guard-bear didn't understand any of this. He simply grunted irritably and butted her forward with his snout.

'All right, have it your own way. But don't expect me to fetch a decent price looking like an unmade bed.'

Doctor Calcupod was at the door, reading the

numbers from their arms as they came out. Beside her, Clericus dutifully wrote them down in the bulky, primrose-coloured scratch-pad that Lectern was holding open.

'More keep-records?' sneered the watching Inspector Dictatum.

Doctor Calcupod merely smiled. 'A pad for thing-every, and thing-every in a pad,' she replied quietly.

Benjamin found himself in the queue for one of a number of waiting carts. They each looked like large cages on wheels – which is exactly what they were. Ahead, Mops and Spike had reached the front of the queue and were already being pushed up a short flight of steps. Beside them, Benjamin saw as he drew nearer, stood a shortish, fattish bear with a bunch of keys tied round his middle. He was talking to Inspector Dictatum.

'Usual ask-prices, Sir?'

Inspector Dictatum nodded, pointing an ugly claw. 'Yes, Sham. Except...sap-that.'

Benjamin was almost at the front of the queue. The claw was pointing at him.

'The hair-red, Sir?' he heard Sham say.

'Yes, Sham. For that-sap is the ask-price...'

Benjamin didn't hear the rest. At that moment he was roughly shoved up the steps and into the cage-cart. The door clanged shut. Sham climbed up onto his driving seat. A whip cracked. The team of cart-pullers (again, Benjamin couldn't bring himself to look at them) took the strain. And with much rattling and shaking, the cart began to move.

Besides himself, Mops and Spike there were three other children on the cage-cart. Benjamin recognised them all from runaround times. One of them was a short, wiry boy named Lewis whose nose always seemed to need wiping (however many times Mops told him to do something about it). The other two were both girls. Brunhilde was older than Benjamin, and a fair bit bigger. She was crying mournfully in the corner of the cart. The other, named Lizzie, was chattering to her, but looked just as unhappy. Would any of them be capable of joining an escape bid? Benjamin doubted it.

'Do you think we'll get a chance to make a run for it?' he whispered in Spike's ear.

Spike shook his head. 'We can't make a run for it if they don't let us out. And I don't reckon they'll let us out. Not unless we're sold, and then it'll be too late.'

Benjamin tried to keep his spirits up. Perhaps Spike was wrong. Perhaps they'd be let out of the cage-cart and put on display or something. That way it might be possible to run for it while Sham the sale-bear wasn't looking. For now, though, the only thing he could do was wait – and watch.

After being waved out through the forbidding gates of the Howling-Tower, the cage-cart bounced and rattled for a short way before swinging left onto another track. Quiet at first, this track soon became busy with other carts. All were being pulled by sweating sap-teams but only theirs were carrying boys and girls. Many of the carts were brightly-coloured and had bold messages painted on their sides. Mops read a few aloud:

'Wellpick Veg-and-Fruit.'

'Guard-you against burn-sun with Smoothies Snout-Lotion.'

'Pumice Brothers for price-cut sharpen-claws.'

Before they'd left the Howling-Tower, Sham had slotted a sign into place on the cage-cart's roof. Benjamin wondered what it said. 'Sale-Saps', perhaps.

The paw-paths at the side of the track were getting busier too, now. Bears were scurrying along in the same direction, clutching various-sized pouches and baskets.

Soon Spike said glumly, 'Looks like we're here.'

The cage-cart had slowed to pass through a narrow entrance and into a wide, open field. The carts already there had been arranged in back-to-back rows, many with one side folded down so that their wares were displayed in the open.

Benjamin's hopes of escape rose slightly. 'Do you think Sham will let the side of our cart down?' he asked.

'Nope,' sighed Spike. 'I told you. I reckon we stay stuck in here unless one of us is bought. And according to Yelp, that boy with the blotchy face in the cage next to us, that ain't likely to happen.'

Benjamin accepted this. Even though the Howling-Tower guard-bears tried to keep them quiet (Inspector Dictatum had growled menacingly, 'Saps-noisy me-give ache-head!') Spike always seemed to find a way of snatching a quiet word to find out what was going on.

Mops argued. 'Why shouldn't any of us be bought? I, for one, fully expect to be in great demand. I shouldn't be surprised if fights broke out over me.'

Spike simply shook his crop-haired head. 'You'll see,' was all he said.

The cage-cart had arrived at what seemed to be its regular spot in the market. It was on the end of a row, next to the Pumice Brothers cart they'd seen on the way. Its owners were busily laying out their stock of sharpen-claws. As soon as they were ready the Pumice Brothers began their sales calls, trying to attract customers.

'Up-roll, up-roll! Sharpen-claws at prices-unrepeatable! Are-there more-none when gone-these!'

They'd quickly gathered a large crowd. Sharpen-claws were an essential of everyday life. After all, it was to their claws that bears owed their supremacy over blunt-fingered humans. Sharpened to a point, a strong claw could be used for tasks as varied as writing (as with Clericus) and injecting with a sleeping-potion (as Inspector Dictatum had shown). Claws sharpened at their ends could gouge roots from the ground or even tin and coal from rock. Two claws sharpened along their edges could cut the toughest of things. Yes, sharpen-claws were big business – and the Pumice Brothers knew how to sell them.

'Look, rounds-five is worth-this. But asking-me rounds-five? No!' One of the Pumice Brothers held a sharpen-claws aloft as the other kept on with his sales talk.

'Even-not rounds-four asking-we. Or three. Or two. What asking-we? Just round-one! Not-you cheaper-find where-any! On-come, who first-be?'

The Pumice Brothers were immediately swamped by customers waving paws full of rounds. Then, as soon as their happy customers had drifted away with their new sharpen-claws, the two bears unloaded another stack from the recesses of their cart and went through the whole business again.

'Up-roll, up-roll! Sharpen-claws at prices-unrepeatable! Are-there more-none when gone-these!'

Sham operated the Howling-Tower cage-carts quite differently, however. He didn't shout and try to attract customers. In fact, he didn't try to make himself noticed at all. He simply lolled on the ground beside the cart, lazily scratching his back against the hub of one wheel. Only once did he stand up and try some sales patter, and even then it came out as nothing more than a mumble: 'Saps-these bargains-not. But asking-me rounds-fifty?   Rounds-hundred?   No.   Even-not hundreds-five. What asking-me? Rounds-thousand. Yes! Not-you dearer-find where-any. On-come, who first-be? No bear? Enough-fair.'

Laughing quietly to himself, Sham went back to his lolling and scratching. Up in the cage-cart, Spike gave Benjamin a told-you-so look.

'Ridiculous!' scoffed Mops. 'How does he expect to sell us like that?'

Benjamin didn't have an answer. Or, rather, the only answer he had simply didn't make sense. For some reason, Sham didn't want to sell them. But if that was the case, why bring them to the market?

Outside, an aged lady-bear was padding from cart to cart. She looked briefly at the Pumice Brother's stock, shaking her greying head as they made her one offer after another. Finally she turned away and shuffled across to the cage-cart.

'Saps-nice,' she cooed. 'Saps-good.'

Sham struggled upright. 'Not so,' he said. 'Are-they saps-horrible.'

'Sap-that not horrible-look.' The lady-bear was pointing at Spike.

'He is. And sap-that...' Sham was now pointing at Mops, 'mad-you-drive. Squeaks stop-non.'

'What!' screeched Mops. 'Call yourself a sale-bear!'

'See-you?' said Sham.

The lady-bear squinted in through the bars at Benjamin Wildfire. 'A hair-red!'

84

Sham nodded. 'Ah. Him-cost price-top. Rounds-thousand-two.'

Two thousand rounds? Benjamin couldn't believe his ears. Were they the instructions Inspector Dictatum had given Sham before they'd left: 'For that-sap the ask-price must be *double*'?

But why?

'It's almost as if he's been told not to sell us,' he murmured.

'Especially you, matey,' said Spike. 'It doesn't make sense, does it?'

Mops gave the cage bar closest to Sham an angry kick. 'It does if he's an idiot,' she snapped. 'And if he thinks a heap of red hair is worth twice as much as elegance and deportment, then an idiot is what he is!'

'But,' asked Benjamin, 'what if he's only obeying orders?'

'Orders *not* to sell us?' echoed Spike.

'Not for less than a thousand rounds, anyway. Which means we must be worth at least that much to them in some other way.' A thought struck him – from their first conversation with Twelve the trusty-sap. 'What did Twelve say the Howling-Tower's proper name was?'

'Outpost-For Sap-Training, Education, Deployment,' Mops rattled out sharply. 'Except that Inspector Doodlebug, whatever-his-name-is, had turned "Training" into "Trading".'

Spike frowned. 'So if we don't get traded we get...educated?'

Benjamin nodded. That could be the only explanation. In some strange way, it had to be worth more than one thousand rounds to Inspector Dictatum if they underwent his education, whatever it was.

The three friends lapsed into silence as they mulled over this mystery. Around them, the market was closing down. One Pumice Brother was greedily counting their takings while the other packed up their remaining stock.

Sham's stock, of course, was already packed up. Neither did he have any money to count. First to trundle out of the field, the cage-carts headed back to the Howling-Tower.

Market day number one had passed. Just four market days to go. And by the look of it, unless a miracle occurred, there was going to be no way of avoiding Inspector Dictatum's Education (whatever that was).

Benjamin Wildfire didn't believe in miracles, of course.

So it came as a very great surprise to him when a miracle (kind of) did occur...

THE MIRACLE

The miracle didn't occur that night. To save him time in loading them into the cage-cart again next morning, Sham didn't let them out. They slept where they were, and there was nothing miraculous about that. Neither did the miracle occur during their second day at Fleeceham Market. That passed in exactly the same way as the first day. Nor on the third day (which was the same as the second), or the fourth (which was just like the previous three). The miracle, such as it was, occurred on their fifth and last day at the market.

As on every other day, they'd been driven out through the gates of the Howling-Tower and trundled to their spot next to the Pumice Brothers. And, as before, Sham had made no attempt to sell them. The difference (and the miracle, kind of) on this day was that somebody came along who really, really wanted to buy one of them.

It happened just before the market closed. By then Benjamin, Mops and Spike had given up all hope. They knew they were doomed to Inspector Dictatum's

'Education' and were sitting, silently and miserably, on the straw-strewn floor of the cage-cart.

That's when a young she-cub scampered up and cried, 'Mama! Papa! Saps!'

The cub's smiling father loped across to join his daughter. He nuzzled her affectionately. The cub's mother (who'd really been more interested looking at the special offers for Smoothies Snout-Lotion) came over as well.

'Full-delight!' said Mother. 'The pinky-dressed is sap-pretty.'

Hearing this, Mops summoned up some sort of a smile. 'True,' she said. 'But you should see me when I'm really made up.'

'Prefer-me the sap-beefy,' said Father, pointing at Spike. 'But need-him exercise-lots!'

'And you'd need rounds-lots to get me, matey,' muttered Spike.

That's when it happened. The miracle.

Having virtually given up hope of anything happening, Benjamin Wildfire had made himself a small, straw cocoon so that he could shed a tear without anybody seeing him. Now, hearing his friends' voices, he peeped sadly out to see what was going on. The moment he did, the she-cub let out a squeal of joy.

'Look-you! A hair-red, Mama!'

'Yes, heart-sweet.'

'Like-just the hair-red saw-we, Papa!'

'Saw-we?' frowned her father. 'When?'

'When went-we to the Hide-Park!'

Benjamin couldn't control himself. He leapt to his feet. Gripping the bars of the cage-cart, he began jumping up and down in wild delight.

'Hide-Park!' he screamed. 'Did you hear that? They've been to Hide-Park! It exists, Mops! Spike, it really exists! Hide-Park exists!'

Of course the bear family didn't understand a word of this. They simply thought it was the way Benjamin Wildfire usually behaved.

'Is-him one-excitable!' exclaimed Father.

'Care-me-not!' squealed the she-cub. 'Can have-me-him, Papa?'

Father scratched his snout. He looked at Mother. Mother rolled her eyes and shrugged her rump in a way that said, 'if that-what wants-she...'.

Father undid the flap of the large pouch hanging round his neck. Out came a paw full of rounds. 'Much-how for hair-red?' he asked.

Sham didn't even move from his spot in the shade beside the front wheel. 'Rounds-thousand-two,' he said in a bored growl.

Father made a noise like a small explosion. 'Rounds-thousand-two? Is-that full-disgrace!'

'True,' agreed Sham.

'Please, Papa!' squealed the she-cub. 'Will be-me good-gold!'

Father inspected his pouch. He did some sums in his head. He sighed, then said to Sham, 'Well-very. Buy-we him.'

Hearing this, Mops and Spike moved close to Benjamin, as if wanting to make the most of their final few moments together. As for Benjamin, he almost thrust his head through the cage-cart bars in his eagerness to see what Sham did next. And what he saw him do next was – nothing. The sale-bear remained lolling beside the cage-cart wheel as he said, 'Oops. Mistaken-me. Hair-red is rounds-thousand-four. What say-you to that?'

'Bye-good!' snapped the father-bear, just beating the mother-bear to it.

As he watched them drag their howling daughter away, Benjamin didn't know whether to be happy or sad.

In a way he was sad they hadn't bought him. It would have been easier to escape from the she-cub's den than from the Howling-Tower, he was fairly certain of that. He was also sad that their five market-days were up, because he suspected that when Inspector Dictatum's education began (whatever that was) he was going to feel a lot sadder.

But at the same time part of him felt wonderfully, joyfully happy. Hide-Park existed! There really was such a place. That bear family had actually been there! It wasn't make-believe, like Spike's awful Mincer, it was real! Mops and Spike had to believe him now.

They did, too. As the cage-cart began its final

journey back to the dark and dreadful shadows of the Howling-Tower they both stayed close to Benjamin and whispered: 'We want to get to Hide-Park, Benjamin. If we ever get out of the Howling-Tower, promise you'll take us with you to find it.'

Benjamin said, 'I promise.'

If we ever get out of the Howling-Tower, was what he thought.

MOUTH-ZERO-IN

Under the watchful eye of Doctor Calcupod, Clericus placed solid ticks in the IN column of the primrose-coloured scratch-pad Lectern was holding aloft for him. He then stepped back, admiring how exactly the ticks matched those he'd made in the OUT column just five days before.

'Complete-register, Doctor Calcupod,' Clericus piped smarmily.

Doctor Calcupod nodded. 'You-thank, Clericus.' He turned to a waiting, and glowering, Inspector Dictatum. 'All correct-present, Inspector.'

'Can-me that-see,' growled the huge bear. He waved an impatient paw at the two guard-bears waiting with him. 'Up-them-lock!'

After days in the cramped and horrible cage-cart, being back in their own cage felt like luxury. Benjamin, Mops and Spike spent a little while walking backwards and forwards, stretching their legs, before they settled down. That night even Inspector Dictatum's ferociously noisy inspections couldn't wake them. They only stirred when the grating of the sap-flap being winched up told them it was sun-come.

By the time they came back inside from runaround, the cage-block was smelling strongly of the soapberry and pine-cone solution that Twelve used for corridor-washing. Sure enough, it wasn't long before they heard the rattle of an empty bucket and the trusty-sap shuffled past. It was the first time they'd seen him since their return from Fleeceham Market.

'Ah, you're back,' he said to nobody in particular. 'Thought you would be.'

Spike had already burrowed into his straw bed. 'Why?' he asked.

'Just going on past form,' sniffed Twelve. 'There hasn't been a human sold in ages.'

'Well, I said I wasn't looking my best!' said Mops sharply. 'And anyway, Benjamin very nearly *was* sold, even at the ridiculous price being asked! He would have been too, if that idiot Sham hadn't then doubled his price again. So there, what do you say to that?'

Twelve said nothing. Mops's little speech seemed to have affected him deeply. For some moments he stood, misty-eyed, in a world of his own. Then, looking at Benjamin he murmured softly, 'Red hair. Just like her...'

'What are you on about now?' asked Mops.

'Nothing, nothing.'

But Mops wasn't to be easily put off. 'Who do you know with red hair? A human? A human who was sold?'

Twelve sighed, then nodded slowly. 'As far as I know, the only human who *has* been sold since Inspector Dictatum took over. Somebody kept offering more and more, however much Sham asked. In the end he had to sell her.'

'*Her*?' Mops let out a cry of triumph. 'Of course! If you want the best, find yourself a female! What was her name? Millicent?'

'Alicia,' admitted Twelve, looking guiltily at Benjamin. 'Alicia…Wildfire.'

Benjamin sat bolt upright. 'Alicia Wildfire? But you said you'd never heard of an Alicia Wildfire!'

'It was a long time ago!' cried Twelve, embarrassed. 'And who's to say she was your mother, anyway?'

'Red hair?' growled Spike. 'Right first name, right last name? Sounds pretty likely, matey.'

Benjamin's mind was spinning with questions. Had his mother also left the farm after Mrs Haggard had taken him away? Had she been caught, looking for him? And sold at Fleeceham Market? Who'd bought her? And…had she been alone? Benjamin gripped the bars of his cage, thrusting his face as close to Twelve as he could. 'Was she in here with a man named Duncan?'

'I can't remember!' snapped Twelve. 'And even if she was, and even if she was your mother, it wouldn't do you any good. You *haven't* been sold. Which means you're down for…'

'We know,' said Benjamin. 'Education, education, education – whatever that is.'

'Will you listen to me!' hissed the trusty-sap. 'It's not "E" for Education. Not any more. That was the old way, before Inspector Dictatum came – like it used to be "T" for "Training" and he turned it into "T" for "Trading".'

'Even though he only sells for ridiculous prices,' Mops couldn't resist pointing out.

'That's because selling us humans ain't the only way of making money,' said Twelve.

The way Twelve said this sent a shiver of fear through Benjamin. 'So what does "E" stand for if it isn't "Education"?'

Twelve took a deep breath. 'Experiments,' he said finally. 'The sort that produce formulas. Formulas are worth a lot of money, y'know.'

'What sort of formulas?' demanded Mops.

'Formulas for lotions and potions.'

Benjamin understood at once. His time with Mrs Haggard had taught him all he needed to know about lotions and potions. 'Like formulas for lotions that stop them getting wrinkly snouts, Mops. Formulas for potions that make them bigger and rounder...'

'Formulas for what to drop in the Mincer for the tastiest sap-sages,' said Spike solemnly.

'I told you never to say that word again!' Mops screeched.

'Formulas for wash-fur lotions that don't make their

eyes sting,' Benjamin said, quickly changing the subject back to what he knew was real. 'There are hundreds of lotions and potions, Mops. They must all have formulas.'

Twelve nodded. 'The bears discovered long ago that different roots and leaves are good for things like aching bones and sore claws. But now they're looking for ones that keep them young or make them prettier. It's not easy, though. Finding the best formula for mixing 'em together takes a lot of – well, working out...'

'And they work these formulas out by testing them on the likes of *us*?' demanded Mops of Twelve. 'How *dare* they? Even us humans have rights, you know. Not many, I know—'

'Well they do!' interrupted Twelve. 'But don't ask me for details. The experiments are all carried out in the secret caverns. Only official-bears are allowed in there. And most humans refuse to talk about it when they come back.' He gave a deep sigh, then added, 'If they come back.'

'If?' Mops's voice rose to a high-pitched squeal. 'What do you mean, *if*? Are you saying some *don't* come back?'

'Not if they're put down for "Mouth-Zero-In" they don't. Get put down for that and the chances are I'll never see 'em ag—'

He didn't finish, for at that moment the door at the far end of the corridor was flung open. Snatching up his bucket and brush, Twelve hurried that way. As he drew near to Doctor Calcupod (for that's who'd just arrived) the trusty-sap fell to his knees. He bowed twice then, still bowing, crawled past her to the door where swift kicks from both Clericus and Lectern sent him on his way.

Doctor Calcupod now began moving slowly down the corridor. Behind her, Clericus had his inky writing-claw poised. Beside him, Lectern was even more burdened than usual. Not only was the assistant weighed down by the same scarlet-covered scratch-pad as on Doctor Calcupod's previous visit, this time he also had a number of oblong signs dangling from his waist. Whenever she stopped at a cage Doctor Calcupod would detach one of these signs from Lectern's collection, hanging it on the bars while Clericus made a note of what it said.

'Can you read any of those signs, Mops?' whispered Benjamin.

Mops pushed her face against the bars of their cage and peered along what she could see of the corridor. 'One says "Sniffle-cures" she murmured. 'And...yes, one says "Wrinkle-stops"...and...'

Mops quickly pulled her head back. Doctor Calcupod was padding their way. Within moments she was peering through the bars at them.

'Suppose-me should-these together-go,' said the sharp-snouted bear with a shake of her head. She gave Benjamin a lingering look. 'Though love me to out-find where-from-comes hair-red. But,' she sighed, 'what-wants Inspector Dictatum, must-get Inspector Dictatum.'

And with that she took three identical signs from around Lectern's waist and hooked them onto the bars of their cage. Clericus duly scratched a record of the decision.

Benjamin waited until they'd moved away, then leaned out and turned one of the signs round. 'Can you read what it says, Mops?' he asked hesitantly.

No answer.

'Mops? Mops?'

'She's fainted,' said a trembling Spike.

Benjamin gulped. He looked at the stricken Mops, laying crumpled on the floor of the cage. He looked at the sign, dangling from its hook.

And, even though he couldn't read, Benjamin had no doubts whatsoever about what it said.

'Mouth-Zero-In'.

THE
FORMULATIONS-CAVERN

Neither Benjamin nor Spike, nor the now-recovered Mops, knew *exactly* what 'Mouth-Zero-In' meant, but they had their suspicions.

'It must mean they don't give us anything to eat,' said Benjamin.

'Well that can only be a blessing,' sniffed Mops, showing that she was well and truly back to normal.

'I wouldn't be so sure about that, matey,' said Spike. 'Better something not-very-nice to eat than nothing to eat at all.'

But that's just what they received. When the sap-flaps lifted for their sun-come feed they heard bowls being removed and returned throughout the cage-block. For Benjamin, Mops and Spike though, there was nothing. Their own bowl stayed put – and empty.

'I don't want to starve!' wailed Mops.

'Told you, didn't I?' grunted Spike.

Mops glared at him. 'I hate you when you're right!'

They were to get no time to bicker about it further. The door at the end of the corridor was suddenly thrust open. Clericus and Lectern marched importantly in, accompanied by a squad of beefy guard-bears.

Their cage's heavy front grille was unlocked and heaved open. Benjamin, Mops and Spike were hauled out. The same thing was happening all the way along the corridor. As each boy or girl was pushed past him, Clericus placed a nice big tick in the scarlet scratch-pad Lectern was holding. Then, flanked by the squad of guard-bears, they were led out into the fresh air and made to line up in double-file. Clericus immediately strode to the head of this column, while Lectern remained sulkily at the rear.

'Tooo...the formulations-cavern!' cried Clericon.

They set off. Although his stomach was churning with fear (and hunger), Benjamin's eyes were working overtime. This was an opportunity to spy out the land and, perhaps, come up with some plan for using his earlier discovery about Inspector Dictatum's nightly routine.

They'd been led from their cage-block out onto a wide dirt track. Risking a glance behind, Benjamin saw that the track ran straight from the Howling-Tower's huge front gates. As for where it led – that he couldn't tell. The track seemed to end at another gate in the distance, but whether there was more beyond it Benjamin had no way of knowing.

He decided to concentrate on what was close at hand. On their right was the cage-block they'd just left.

They'd been brought out through the end door and they were being marched alongside it. He soon saw the upper branches of the runaround-yard tree peeping over the block's flat roof.

Now it got much more interesting. They were passing a dumpy, dome-shaped building. This was connected to the cage-block, but sticking out from it in such a way as to make it impossible to see from the runaround-yard. It had no door, just an open entrance with an unlit lantern on a hook beside it. Benjamin peered through the dark and gloomy opening but had time to see no more than a silvery glint in one corner before they'd been marched by.

Another mystery immediately presented itself. Attached to the dumpy, dome-shaped building was a huge, round wheel, like the wheel of the cage-cart. Benjamin gave Mops a gentle nudge with his elbow.

'What do you reckon that is?' he hissed.

'A very tacky decoration?' sniffed Mops. 'Some bears have no taste.'

'Silence!' bellowed Lectern (determined that nobody was going to forget about him, just because he was at the back of the procession).

On they went. Past cage-block after identical cage-block, each with its own runaround-yard and dome-shaped attachment and tacky, decorative wheel. Could this be the route that Inspector Dictatum follows every night? Benjamin wondered. As we march along tomorrow, he decided, I'll see what I can count up to. Only then did he think: if there *is* a tomorrow...

At the head of the procession, Clericus swung sharply to his left. He was now leading them down a narrow path towards what looked like the smallest cave in the whole of the Howling-Tower. It had an equally small door, with a small spy-hole set into it.

Clericus stopped. Lectern bustled forward with the scarlet ledger, heaving it open as Clericus played a complicated rap on the door. A small shutter slid back. One eye appeared, with a bit of a blue-black snout. They heard a muffled demand of 'Give the word-pass!'

'Password!' said Clericus importantly.

Benjamin felt cold and frightened. Beside him, Mops shivered and gave a nervous little squeak. Behind them, Spike stayed bravely silent. So, too, did many of the others who'd been marched there with them, although many just couldn't stop themselves whimpering with fear.

The door-bear had obviously heard what he wanted to hear. The spy-hole snapped shut. The small door swung open to admit Clericus and Lectern. Now the queue began to shuffle forward. The two trembling girls at the front were called through. The door closed again. After a short delay it opened to admit a couple of terrified boys. And so it went on, with the queue being dealt with in twos and threes as dictated by Clericus. Then, all too soon, the heavy door was creaking open to receive Benjamin, Mops and Spike. A guard-bear thrust them forward. They heard the door slam shut behind them with a solid, echoing thud, as if it had no intention of ever opening again.

Doctor Calcupod was waiting for them. She was perched behind a desk made from a stone slab. Laid out on the slab were lines of identical, brand-new, purple-covered scratch-pads. Humming to herself, Doctor Calcupod found the one she was looking for. She handed it to Lectern to hold.

'Tatting experiment, session-first,' she purred. 'Specimens F1, F2 and F3.'

Clericus dipped his writing-claw into a fresh pot of ink and lovingly scratched down the details.

This done, Doctor Calcupod turned towards an alcove beside the slab desk. Now she spoke sharply. 'Need-me Quantity-Counting Assistants!'

Two burly she-bears immediately bustled out from the alcove, wiping their snouts and brushing crumbs from their fronts. Each wore an armband carrying the initials QCA.

'Conduct heavy-count,' ordered Doctor Calcupod. 'First-him.'

With the QCAs at each arm, Benjamin was dragged across to a large contraption with two baggy pouches hanging from a wooden frame. One QCA lifted him bodily and dropped him in one of the pouches. At the same time the second QCA dropped a great, heavy stone into the other pouch. Benjamin's seat shot alarmingly downwards, only to shoot just as quickly up again as the stone-handling QCA lobbed more of them into the other pouch. After lurching sickeningly up and down a few times, Benjamin's pouch finally settled into a steady position.

Doctor Calcupod stepped forward to examine the contents of the pouch.

'Stones six, pebbles eleven,' she announced, and Clericus recorded.

Mops and Spike then went through exactly the same performance until Doctor Calcupod announced the numbers for Clericus to add to the new purple scratch-pad.

'What was all that about?' whispered Mops once it was over.

Spike shrugged, but Benjamin had remembered something from the dark days he'd spent with Mrs Haggard.

'They're testing how heavy we are. Mrs Haggard used to do it all the time. She had a plank across a log. She'd roll a big boulder on one end of the plank, then step on the other end. If the boulder didn't move, it always put her in a bad mood for some reason.'

This final word was almost drowned out by the start of a clanking, grinding noise – just like the noise of a sap-flap opening, only much louder. There was a reason for this. Something like a sap-flap, but much larger, was being winched open. At a signal from Doctor Calcupod, the wall beside her slab desk had begun to move upwards. The awful truth of the formulations-cavern was about to be revealed.

NOURISHMENT-FAILURE

Pushed forward by the QCAs, Benjamin, Mops and Spike found themselves on a narrow balcony. A wobbly metal rail was all that stood between them and a terrifying plunge – because what they now saw was that most of the formulations-cavern was below ground level.

Benjamin could hardly bear to look. The whole, vast area was divided into small cubicles. And housed in each cubicle was a lonely, frightened-looking human. Most were boys or girls, though a few were adults.

'Specimens for fatting-experiment,' called Doctor Calcupod to the QCA who was already scurrying up some metal stairs towards them.

'Cubicles waiting-ready, Doctor Calcupod.'

'Good-very. Them-install, then orders-wait.'

Benjamin, Mops and Spike were marched down onto the cavern floor and across to a group of three empty cubicles arranged in a triangle facing inwards. Benjamin was pushed into one cubicle, Mops into the second and Spike into the third. They were each held down on small stools while their ankles were quickly manacled to iron rings set into the floor. In front of each stool was a bare, wooden table.

Clericus ticked a column in Lectern's purple scratch-pad. 'Fatting-potion specimens installed-all.' A QCA hurried off to inform Doctor Calcupod.

'What's a fatting-potion?' whispered Spike to Mops.

'I haven't the slightest idea,' replied Mops, then she looked at Benjamin. His face had gone a deathly white. 'You – you *know*, don't you?'

Benjamin nodded. He'd also worked out why Mrs Haggard always ended up in a bad mood after standing on her log-plank.

'Well, tell us!' squawked Mops. 'Is a potion the same as a lotion?'

'No. Lotions are what bears rub on. Potions are what they swallow.'

Spike moaned. 'They're gonna get us to swallow a potion. That's why we haven't had anything to eat.'

'He said *fatting*-potion,' repeated Mops urgently. 'What's that?'

'It's a potion for making bears bigger and fatter,' said Benjamin. 'Some of Mrs Haggard's potions were fatting-potions, I'm sure they were. She'd take a spoonful, then go and stand on her log-plank to see if she'd become fat enough to make the boulder on the other end go up in the air. But she never did – because the fatting-potion never worked. *That's* what must have made her so angry.'

107

'Quiet-be!' shouted a QCA, giving Benjamin a cuff round the head before snapping to attention.

Doctor Calcupod was descending the stairs from the balcony. Following behind her was Inspector Dictatum.

'Specimens F1, F2 and F3,' announced Doctor Calcupod once they'd reached the triangle of cubicles. 'Approve-you, Inspector?'

Inspector Dictatum lumbered slowly from cubicle to cubicle. He inspected Mops, who wrinkled her nose in disgust. He inspected Spike, who muttered deep in his throat, 'You're really ugly, matey.'

Then he inspected Benjamin. Closely. So closely that Benjamin could smell the great bear's hot, foul breath and see the nasty brown bits between his evil yellow teeth. A shiver ran down his spine as Inspector Dictatum stepped back and pointed one of his massive claws straight at him.

'Dose-triple for hair-red,' he snarled. Then, pointing at Mops and Spike in turn, 'Dose-double for her. Dose-single for him.'

'As-wish-you, Inspector,' nodded Doctor Calcupod.

'Stir potion-doses into strong-extra blueberry-mixture. Has potion-this taste-bitter. If saps like-not then bears like-not certain-for.

'Yes, Inspector.'

'Carefully heavy-count each sun-come and sun-go.'

'Yes, Inspector.'

'Questions-any?' growled Inspector Dictatum.

Just one keen QCA put up a paw. 'What-if they eat-not-want, Sir? Use-we funnel-tubes?'

'No feed-force!' replied Inspector Dictatum. 'When enough-hungry, eat-they-will.'

'But...' persisted the keen QCA, 'not-they food-get when cage-back?'

'Are-them mouth-zero-in.' Doctor Calcupod said smoothly. 'Swallow-them fatting-potions – or thing-no.'

'More questions-any?' asked Inspector Dictatum impatiently.

Hesitantly, the keen QCA raised her paw again. 'Just er – one thing-final, Sir. Should ready-we-be for a—'

The QCA's question was cut off by a terrible howl of agony coming from the far side of the cavern.

A round-faced boy in a cubicle beneath a big red sign had fallen from his stool and was writhing on the ground clutching his stomach. None of the QCAs were offering him any help. Most were adding notes to little scratch-pads of their own. Only one, rather flustered, QCA was doing something else: he was hurrying in Inspector Dictatum's direction.

'Nourishment-failure, honey-substitute trials, Sir!' cried the QCA.

Inspector Dictatum's eyes narrowed. 'Have-you records-complete?'

'Yes, Sir.'

'Replacement-sap ready-go?'

'Yes, Sir. The experiment continue-can.'

On the far side of the cavern the poor boy's dreadful howls were growing fainter. A sudden, terrible thought came to Benjamin: was this why the bears all called it the Howling-Tower? Slowly the cries from the other side of the formulations-cavern gurgled to a complete stop, leaving behind only a heavy silence.

Inspector Dictatum turned to the QCA who'd run over to him. 'Aware-you of away-pass activity?'

'Yes, Sir,' snapped the QCA smartly. 'Insides-examine to out-find the failure-cause…'

'Correct. Then?'

'Sap-disposal, Sir. Quick-double.'

'Correct. On-carry.'

As the honey-substitute QCA scurried away, Inspector Dictatum turned back to the team responsible for looking after Benjamin, Mops and Spike.

'Note-take,' he said. 'Expect-me efficiency-same if get-you nourishment-failure in experiment-this.'

Instructions given, Inspector Dictatum and Doctor Calcupod went off to tour the cavern's other experiments with Clericus and Lectern trailing dutifully behind them. Pausing only to breathe a sigh of relief that they'd survived the Inspector's inspection, the QCAs now scurried away themselves.

In his cubicle, Benjamin was thinking hard. Inspector Dictatum had said that what had happened to the round-faced boy in the honey-substitute experiment could happen to them too. But what exactly *had* happened?

He looked across at Spike and Mops – like him, manacled and seated in their cubicles. 'What do you think a 'nourishment-failure' is?' he hissed.

'I don't care what it is!' cried Mops, panic-stricken. 'If it makes me howl like that poor boy then I don't want to know!'

'Let's face it,' said Spike miserably. 'You heard them: sap-disposal. One way or the other we're on the way to the Mincer.'

'Do not say that word!' screeched Mops. 'There's no such thing!'

Benjamin was looking over at the honey-substitute experiment area. A big red sign was hanging above the cubicles there.

'Turn round, Mops,' he urged. 'Can you read what that sign says?'

Mops twisted on her stool. She stared silently at the sign. When she turned back again, she could hardly force the words out.

'It's a warning to the help-bears,' she squeaked, quivering with fear. 'It says: "Poison-Danger! Paws-Wash!"'

'Poison?' gasped Benjamin. 'That's what they call a nourishment-failure? One of us being poisoned?'

So that was why the assistants had been more interested in taking notes than in doing anything to help. Finding out if a potion was poisonous was all part of the experiment – because if a potion was poisonous to saps, then perhaps it would be poisonous to bears. Not a very good selling point!

'It won't happen to us, will it?' cried Mops. 'It can't! It mustn't!'

'I reckon it will,' said Spike.

Mops glared at him, her tear-filled eyes flashing defiantly. 'Oh, you're such a misery! Why can't you ever look on the bright side?'

Spike simply pointed upwards. Above their little triangle of cubicles hung a sign. A red sign reading (saw Mops, while Benjamin and Spike simply knew) 'Poison-Danger! Paws-Wash!'

'Oh,' said Mops, dumbstruck.

Benjamin couldn't even manage that. He was too busy staring at the table in front of him. It was no longer bare. Neither were the tables in front of Spike and Mops. The QCAs had returned with special formulations-cavern food bowls. They were full to overflowing.

BOWLS OF PLENTY

'Don't touch it!' hissed Benjamin.

'I have absolutely no intention of touching it,' said Mops. 'I wouldn't touch it even if it looked delicious, which it most certainly does not.'

Benjamin wasn't so sure about that. Compared to the muddle of berries, acorns, roots, leaves and gristly meaty bits they were usually served, what was in the bowl before him looked really tasty. It held a golden-brown layer of crusty stuff. The crusty stuff had a small slit in the centre. Out of this slit wafted a plume of steam carrying a quite delightful aroma of hot, sugared blueberries. Some fruits are enjoyed just as much by humans as they are by bears, and crafty Inspector Dictatum knew that the blueberry is one of them. Benjamin's mouth began to water. His head began to dip towards the bowl...

'So don't touch any yourself!' yelled Spike.

Benjamin jerked his head back just in time. Not very far, though. 'Surely one little taste won't hurt?'

'How d'you know?' demanded Spike. 'One little taste

might be all it takes. And even if it ain't poisonous, it still ain't likely to do us any good. If it works, we could explode instead.'

'Explode?' echoed Mops. Her eyes opened saucer-wide. 'You're saying that a fatting-potion could make us get fatter and fatter until…'

'Your skin can't stretch no more,' nodded Spike grimly. 'Then – bang!'

Spike was right, realised Benjamin. They couldn't afford to take even the tiniest taste. He sat back and turned his head away from the delicious blueberry smells. 'I am not going to give in,' he said firmly.

'Nor am I,' said Mops.

'Nor am I,' said Spike, staring at his bowl of blueberry pie. He sighed. 'I'm not gonna give in…even though I'm hungry…really, really hungry…and this looks so nice…'

'Tell yourself it doesn't!' cried Mops. 'Tell yourself it looks completely disgusting!' But even as she spoke, her own nose was twitching and sniffing. 'Well, fairly disgusting…all right then, slightly… disgustingly…yummy…ooh, it smells yummy, it really does, oooh…'

'STOP!' yelled Benjamin at the top of his voice.

QCAs from all over the formulations-cavern swung Benjamin's way. One of the fatting-potion QCAs moved threateningly towards him, ready to cuff him round the ear if he didn't stop his noise at once. But his desperate shout had worked. Startled, both Mops and Spike had again jerked away from their food bowls. Like him they were now sitting as far back on their stools as possible, their noses turned away from the tempting blueberry smells.

'Every time one of us looks like we might be going to take a bite, the others must shout,' said Benjamin.

'Even if it means we get hit,' urged Mops.

'Better do it loudly, mateys,' said Spike, "cos I don't know how long I'm gonna be able to hold out.'

Gritting their teeth and scrunching their noses, the three friends tried to take their minds off blueberries by watching the passage of the sun through the frosted panels of the cavern's roof. They watched it start on one side. They watched it creep oh-so-slowly across the sky until, with their mouths watering and their stomachs rumbling horribly, they saw it disappear from view – and they heard a bell jangle.

Immediately, a Quantity-Counting Assistant scurried over and took away their food bowls. Each (as Clericus noted on his purple scratch-pad) was still as full as when they'd first been put in front of them. Not a scrap had passed their lips. They'd done it!

Benjamin, Mops and Spike were then released from their manacles. They were led up the iron stairs to be put in the weighing pouches again. Then, once more under guard, the three friends began the return trek to their cage-block.

Benjamin's thoughts were a jumble. They'd survived their first day in the formulations-cavern – unlike the many who Twelve had said that he never saw again. But how many more days would they be able to hold out, before hunger so overwhelmed them that they gulped down the fatting-potions and poisoned themselves (or exploded)?

It would be a question the three friends would ask themselves repeatedly. As they resisted the blueberry mixture the next day, the blueberry mixture with a wonderful raspberry topping the day after, and then the same concoction with mouth-wateringly juicy loganberries sprinkled over it the day after, Benjamin, Mops and Spike grew gradually weaker. At the end of their fourth day without food, they didn't so much march back to their cages as totter. It was Mops who took Benjamin's mind off how feeble he felt, by drawing something other than food to his attention.

'Now, guess what that's just reminded me of.'

They'd reached the first of the cage-blocks, with its dumpy, dome-shaped extension. Mops, a pace behind Benjamin, was pointing at the strange decorative cartwheel thing attached to its side.

'What?'

'My wheely-box!'

Beside Benjamin, Spike groaned. 'Not again, please!'

'What do you mean, not again?' Mops bristled. 'I haven't mentioned it for ages. And even if I have...'

116

'You have,' said Spike.

'It's because that wheely-box was my own personal private property. It should be here, with me!'

It was a grumble Benjamin had heard many times, ever since he'd told Mops his fuzzy memory of coming round in the Howling-Tower and hearing Inspector Dictatum's bellow: 'Sap-things to the store-cave!"

This news had not pleased Mops. 'My wheely-box shut away in a store-cave? It's a disgrace, an absolute disgrace! How can I keep myself looking in peak condition if all my accoutrements have been confiscated?'

Usually Benjamin would switch off and let Mops moan on. After all, he'd lost his own bag as well, hadn't he? But now, as Benjamin's stomach gave an empty rumble, he remembered something about his bag that was vitally, vitally important. It contained the supplies he had managed to snaffle while Mrs Haggard was out of the way. It contained food!

'Mops!' hissed Benjamin. 'What did your wheely-box have in it?'

'Essentials, of course. Spare ribbons, nail file, clean socks...'

'To eat, I mean!'

'Oh, hardly anything. A few loaves-crusty, a couple of dozen bars-chewy, stacks of fruits-dried and bags of treats-tasty. Just enough to keep us going for ten days or so.'

'Ten days!'

'All right, fifteen,' shrugged Mops. 'What difference does it make?'

'Obvious, ain't it?' said Spike from behind them. 'With your wheely-box we'd have enough food to hold out for a while. We wouldn't be so tempted by the fatting-potion.'

'Well I haven't got it, have I?' Mops gave a tearful sniff. 'My lovely case is shut away in some store-cave getting dirtier and grimier. Oh, it's so unfair! That case was my pride and joy. The time I spent polishing and buffing those wheels!'

Spike sniffed. 'Shiny, were they?'

'Shiny? You could have seen those wheels in a hole-coal at middle-night!'

Or, realised Benjamin suddenly, in the darkest corner of a dumpy, dome-shaped building...

'Mops!' he cried, 'I think I've seen them!'

'What? Where?'

An irritated roar from a guard-bear stopped Benjamin from saying more than a quick, 'Wait. I'll show you.'

They'd already marched over half the distance back to their cage-block, past other identical blocks with their own dome-shaped buildings. As they plodded on, Benjamin tried to get a look at what was inside them, but they were all far too dark to see a thing. Had his imagination played tricks on him? His confidence began to fade.

They were nearly there. The next cage-block was

theirs. He could see the upper branches of the runaround-yard tree. He could see the decorative wheel attached to the side of the dumpy, dome-shaped building. And soon...

'There! Look!'

It was still there, just as he'd remembered seeing it on their first morning's march to the formulations-cavern: a circular, spangly object, twinkling in the darkness of the dome-shaped building's interior, like a distant star.

'My wheels!' cried Mops, at once. 'I'd know them anywhere!'

Benjamin felt a soaring hope. They knew where the store-cave was! They knew where Mops's wheely-box (and his own bag, probably) had been thrown. They knew where a food supply was to be found!

And, as he looked up above the store-cave's dome-shaped roof, Benjamin suddenly also knew how they might be able to get hold of it.

THE STRENGTH TEST

After they'd been dumped back in their cages, it was soon time for sun-go runaround. Benjamin scurried outside as quickly as his weakened legs would let him. He wanted to check his idea. By the time Mops and Spike joined him, he was pointing excitedly up into the tree in the yard.

'See that branch? The thick one that forks in the middle?'

'What about it?' said Spike.

'It nearly reaches as far as the cage-block roof, that's what,' Benjamin said. 'I can't believe I didn't notice it before.'

Spike looked up from his usual seat on the round rock. The thick branch Benjamin was showing them did indeed reach out across the runaround-yard's fence of unbreakable wire and viciously spiky top to end close to the cage-block's low, flat roof – but a fair way above it.

'So?'

'So somebody could get on that branch, crawl along

120

it, jump down onto the cage-block roof, run across to the store-cave roof, slide safely down the dome to the ground, grab some food out of Mops's wheely-box and come back with it!'

Spike and Mops looked at Benjamin, then at each other. 'You're mad,' said Mops finally.

'No, I'm not,' said Benjamin. 'It could work!'

'How would they get up this tree in the first place?' said Spike, pointing at the first reachable branch well above their heads.

'Climb the fence and jump across,' said Benjamin (hopefully).

'And how do they get back again?' asked Mops.

'Same way they went,' said Benjamin.

Mops arched one eyebrow. 'Carrying heavy food? My owner didn't skimp, you know. We're talking quality loaves-crusty here.'

'They don't carry the food. First they come round and lob it over the fence for the other two to catch.'

Spike shook his head. 'During a runaround time? With guards watching?'

'No. At night. When there's only Inspector Dictatum on duty.'

'Only!' squawked Mops.

'Not while he's around, of course. After he goes past our cage-block. He always takes a count of two thousand two hundred and twelve before he comes back again.'

'He does?' said Spike.

'He does,' said Benjamin – and explained how he knew.

Once again, Mops and Spike looked at each other. Again they looked at Benjamin Wildfire.

'And then we'd have some grub to eat?' said Spike.

'Yes!' nodded Benjamin enthusiastically.

'And I'd get my nail file back?' asked Mops.

'Yes!'

'You've thought of everything?' said Mops.

Benjamin quickly ran the plan through in his mind once more: fence, branch, higher branch, roof, slide down, store-cave, food, throw over, climb up, roof, branch, lower branch, fence. Only then did he answer, in a voice that had sunk from one of high excitement to a miserable whisper: 'No. I've forgotten something.'

'What?' asked Spike.

'We'll have been shut in our cages for the night. So unless we can work out how to lift our sap-flap, the plan can't even start.'

'I don't see why we have to lift our sap-flap,' frowned Mops.

'Because it's the only way out, stupid!' cried Benjamin furiously.

Tears of frustration pricked at his eyes. Lifting a sap-flap wasn't possible. He'd tried, often. The sap-flap had never budged a fraction.

'I am not stupid,' said Mops coldly, hands on hips.

'You are if you don't see why we have to lift our sap-flap,' Benjamin retorted.

'If that's your opinion,' sighed Mops, 'then I refuse to discuss the matter further. But I still don't see why we want to go to all the trouble of lifting our sap-flap when the guard-bears do it for us every runaround time. Personally, I'd have thought that what we need to work out is how to *keep* it lifted.'

It was Spike who broke the stunned silence with a whistle of wonderment. 'Matey — that is *brilliant*!'

Benjamin couldn't have put it better himself. After apologising like mad, he started thinking about this different problem. There, in front of his eyes, the cage-block's whole row of sap-flaps were indeed open, clankingly winched up to their highest to let them out for this runaround time. Only when they went back in would those sap-flaps fall shut with an echoing clang. But if something got in the way to stop them shutting...

There wasn't a moment to lose. The two powerful guard-bears were already marching in step towards the far end of the cage-block, a sure sign that runaround time was almost at an end.

'Quick!' he shouted. 'Think of something we could put beneath the flap.'

'Such as?' asked Mops. 'We're hardly awash with fixtures and fittings.'

She was right. Their straw bedding certainly

wouldn't do the trick. Nor would their food or water bowls be strong enough.

'We need something solid,' said Benjamin urgently.

'Pity we're down as mouth-zero-in, then,' said Mops. 'You could have used our supper. That's usually as hard as a rock.'

Benjamin laughed in delight. 'Mops, you've done it again!' he shouted. 'Spike, get up. We need your rock!'

There wasn't a moment to lose. Heaving and laughing, as if they were playing a silly game, Benjamin and Spike began rolling the heavy rock towards their open sap-flap. Beside the fence, Mops danced a little jig so as to attract the attention of the two guard-bears marching along outside the runaround-yard fence.

'We're playing rock and roll!' she trilled.

By the time she'd finished, Benjamin and Spike had pushed the rock safely into their cage. As the klaxon sounded, Mops stopped jigging and raced back to join them. She found Benjamin on his knees beside the opening, the rock between his hands.

Moments later, they heard the distant sound of unwinding chains. Their heavy sap-flap groaned, gave a little jerk, then began to fall.

'Now!' hissed Mops and Spike together.

Benjamin quickly rolled the rock beneath the descending flap. Down it came, rattling and screeching, until with a clank and a dong – it stopped.

Up and down the cage-block they could hear

sap-flaps falling that little bit further, making the floor shudder as they slammed fully down. But – not theirs! Benjamin bent lower to inspect things. The rock had been slightly chipped, but no more. It hadn't been cracked. And it had stopped the door!

Benjamin peered out through the wonderful, marvellous gap at the bottom of his sap-flap. He could see that night had fallen on the Howling-Tower. He could see the runaround-yard. And, beyond the runaround-yard fence, he could see Inspector Dictatum getting ready to begin his rounds.

'I can see Inspector Dictatum!' he cried.

'But...' said Spike slowly. 'If you can see him – don't that mean he can see you?'

WISH ME LUCK

Inspector Dictatum was already coming their way. Benjamin could hear his chuffs and puffs which would very soon become hisses, growls and roars. Unable to look away, Benjamin could see the great bear's claws shimmering in the moonlight. He could see his teeth, shining like daggers. And, worst of all, he could soon see the glint of Inspector Dictatum's flickering eyes.

He'd stopped. Standing stock-still, beyond the runaround-yard fence, he was looking directly at the jammed-open sap-flap. Benjamin shrank back into the corner of his cage and waited for the worst.

Sure enough, Inspector Dictatum hissed – loudly. He growled – even more loudly. He built up to a more powerful, more shattering roar than Benjamin had ever heard him produce before. And then he moved on, as usual.

'He – he's going away!' cried Benjamin. 'He didn't see me!'

'He'll be back,' said Spike gloomily.

Inspector Dictatum did come back, of course, a count

of two thousand two hundred and twelve later. And again, and again after that. But not once, to Benjamin's great relief, did he spot anything wrong.

Now why should that have been? Why, if Benjamin could see Inspector Dictatum beyond the runaround-yard's high fence, couldn't Inspector Dictatum see Benjamin? The reason is not simply that it's easier to see out to a big space than in to a little space. It's also to do with the fact that, while bears have a wonderful sense of smell, their eyesight isn't quite so hot. With up-close things they're fine. Colours are sharp. They can spot a tasty whitebark pine nut in a bed of leaves without the slightest difficulty. But put a bear rather further away – outside the perimeter fence of a runaround-yard, for example – and he won't be able to tell the dark rustiness of a sap-flap from the dark nothingness of a gap beneath that flap. Only by seeing a face peering out through that gap would the bear be given a clue that something was wrong – and Benjamin Wildfire was far too clever to let him see that.

And so Benjamin's jammed-open sap-flap remained undetected. When the sap-flaps were winched up to their full height for runaround time next morning, Benjamin was able to roll the rock away, cover it with straw, and no bear was any the wiser. Spike and Mops were ecstatic.

'You're a genius!' cried Mops.

'She's not wrong,' said Spike, adding, 'for once.'

Benjamin, proud as he was, got them quickly back to business. Before they were taken off to the formulations-cavern again there were plans to be made.

'Tonight we'll do the same thing again,' he said urgently. 'Then, when Inspector Dictatum has gone past, we'll crawl out and one of us will go up that tree and head for the store-cave. Then he——'

'Or she,' interrupted Mops. 'Just because I'm pretty it doesn't mean I'm all weak and wobbly.'

'All right,' nodded Benjamin. 'When he – or she – gets to the store-cave, he or she dives straight for my bag or Mops's wheely-box. He or she grabs some of the food, tosses it over the fence to the others then tries to get back here before Inspector Dictatum spots him or her and rips him – or her – to shreds.'

'Him,' said Mops firmly. 'I'd be fine for the diving, grabbing and tossing but perfectly hopeless for the ripping to shreds bit.'

Spike laid a hand solemnly on Benjamin's shoulder. 'You know it's got to be you, matey. I wouldn't have the confidence.'

Benjamin nodded. 'You'll both have important jobs to do, anyway.'

'Tonight it is, then,' said Spike. 'So long as we're not poisoned today,' he couldn't resist adding gloomily.

They weren't poisoned that day.

As usual, they were marched under guard to the formulations-cavern, weighed, taken to their cubicles, manacled, seated – and had brimming bowls of their different fatting-potions put in front of them by the Quantity Counting Assistants.

What happened then (as duly recorded by Clericus on Lectern's purple scratch-pad) was that none of them ate a single mouthful.

That's not to say they weren't tempted. They really were. But whenever one of them put a hand anywhere near their food bowl the other two would cry out encouragingly: 'Wait till tonight!'

At the end of the day the QCAs weighed Benjamin, Mops and Spike again. It was noted that Benjamin was now eight pebbles lighter, Mops five pebbles lighter and that Spike's weight had gone down by a full thirteen pebbles. Then they were marched back to their cage-block.

That evening, for the first time ever, they didn't go out for runaround time. They were all too weak anyway, and Benjamin needed to save what little energy he still had. Instead they crouched, the round rock at the ready, beside their open sap-flap. After what seemed an age, they finally heard the tell-tale rattle of chains signalling that the flaps were about to be dropped for the night. The rock was rolled into position. Down came the flap – and stopped.

Benjamin peered outside. Soon Inspector Dictatum

would be starting his rounds. The moment he'd gone past, out they would go. It was time to remind Mops and Spike of their critical role in the operation.

'Now don't forget, Inspector Dictatum's always away for a count of two thousand two hundred and twelve. To be on the safe side give me a whistle when you reach one thousand nine hundred.' Benjamin looked sharply at his two friends as a sudden thought struck him. 'You can count that high?'

'Of course I can count that high,' Mops snorted, 'you don't have to worry about *that*!'

Benjamin soon found enough other things to worry about anyway. Out beyond the runaround-yard fence, Inspector Dictatum seemed to be in one of his angriest moods. Kneeling beside the jammed sap-flap, Benjamin was shaking so much he wondered if he'd be capable of climbing at all.

Slowly and terrifyingly, the chuffs, puffs, hisses, growls and roars grew louder as the great bear headed their way. They peaked as he prowled the length of the runaround-yard fence, causing Benjamin, Mops and Spike to shrink back into the corners of their cage. Then, gradually they began to fade.

'Let's go,' hissed Benjamin.

'I'm with you, matey,' whispered Spike.

Mops started to count. 'One, two, three...'

Crawling out beneath their sap-flap, the three friends scurried silently across the moonlit runaround-yard.

Mops and Spike slipped into the shadow of the tree, while Benjamin dashed past them to the wire fence. Pausing only to make sure he'd got a firm toe-hold, he began to climb.

As Benjamin moved swiftly upwards, the fence creaked and groaned. In the darkness it sounded so loud. Thankfully, a distant, echoing roar from Inspector Dictatum gave him some comfort. The great bear was making so much noise himself that he couldn't possibly be able to hear anything else above it. Benjamin climbed on.

Within moments, he found himself level with the branch which hung above the runaround-yard. Carefully avoiding the vicious barbed coils just above his head, Benjamin thrust out a hand and grabbed it. Thankfully it was as thick and solid as it looked from down on the ground. He took a deep breath. Then, in one rapid movement, he thrust himself away from the fence with his feet, gripped the branch with his other hand and heaved. In an instant he'd looped his body over the branch and was hauling himself upwards!

'Well done!' hissed Spike from below.

'Eighty four, eighty five...' murmured Mops.

Benjamin caught his breath, then crawled along the branch until he'd reached the gnarled trunk of the tree. He got carefully to his feet, peered up, then began climbing again. He didn't stop until he'd reached the vital second branch, the one that stretched out above the fence and across towards the cage-block and the dome-shaped roof of the store-cave. He began to crawl along the branch, swaying slightly as he looked down, and saw the barbed wire directly beneath him. Benjamin crawled further – and saw the wire no more. His heart leapt. He'd crossed the line of the fence!

On he went, ignoring the twigs which bit at his shirt like wooden teeth. The branch was becoming thinner but still held his weight. On he went, until directly beneath him he saw, to his delight, the wide, flat centre of the dome-shaped roof! All he had to do was grip the branch firmly with both hands, lever himself off, dangle in the air, then drop the very short distance onto it.

Which he did.

Only then did he look across and down to where Mops and Spike were huddled together in the shadows of the runaround-yard.

'Wish me luck,' he called, as loudly as he dared.

'Good luck, matey,' Spike's hushed voice floated up.

'Two hundred and twenty, good luck Benjamin, two hundred and twenty-two...' counted Mops.

And with that, Benjamin Wildfire turned away and set out to find the food that would save their lives.

THE STORE-CAVE

Benjamin made a useful discovery almost at once (although exactly how useful he wouldn't realise for some days). Snaking across roof of the cage-block he'd just left were a number of rusting chains. At various points on the roof, groups of these chains had been linked together, eventually leaving only a single, thick chain to snake onwards. (The arrangement reminded Benjamin of how Mops's hair had looked when she'd had ribbons to draw strands of it together into plaits).

This remaining single chain, Benjamin saw, ran round the side of the dome-shaped roof and down to the decorative wheel that Mops disliked so much. At that moment, however, Benjamin thought the whole arrangement was the most wonderful he'd ever seen. By holding on to this chain, he was able to sit and slither down the dome-shaped roof far quicker than he'd expected. Landing on the rim of the decorative wheel, Benjamin had to do no more than climb down it and hop lightly onto the ground.

Three hundred and ten, three hundred and

eleven…Benjamin counted in his head. He'd decided it would be a good idea to try to keep count, so that he'd know roughly how long he'd got before hearing the warning whistle from Mops and Spike.

Darting into the shadows, he flattened himself against the store-cave wall. Side step, side step, side step – and he was there, at the entrance. What's more, the lantern beside it was now lit. Snatching it from its hook, Benjamin dashed inside.

He was met by the saddest sight he'd ever seen. The store-cave was piled high with bags and boxes. And not only those. There were dust-covered heaps of other things that owner-bears would buy or make for their saps. Sap-shoes, gouged and shaped by a carver's claws; sap-clothing, spun from hair or sewn from hides; sap-decorations, like clip-hairs and thin wire rings-for-ears; even favourite sap-toys, such as skip-vines and dolly-cuddles. Each and every one of them owned by a child who'd ended their days here in the Howling-Tower.

Benjamin blinked back the tears in his eyes. There was no time for sorrow. He had to do what he'd come to do. He owed it to Mops and Spike and, in a funny sort of way, to all the owners of the vast collection of things in the store-cave.

Twisting and turning the lantern, Benjamin played its light across the piles of stuff. Only then did he realise that the two things he'd expected to see were missing. To be precise, two spangly wheels. Mops's wheely-box had gone.

Five hundred and seventeen, five hundred and eighteen, chimed the count in Benjamin's head. He tried not to panic.

Forcing himself to take things slowly, Benjamin looked more carefully. He noticed that some of the piles were covered in thick dust and cobwebs as if they'd been there for many moons. But as he moved the light further round, the layers of dust and tangles of cobwebs became thinner. A section in the corner opposite the entrance – the section he must have been able to see as he marched past, realised Benjamin – had hardly any at all. And there could be only one reason for that.

It had to be the section used for the possessions of children captured most recently – those like himself, Mops and Spike. There'd been some new arrivals in their block that very sun-come. He'd heard their crying from the cages at the far end. If he was right, then their stuff would have been tossed onto that same pile. Mops's wheely-box could be buried underneath.

Placing the lantern on the floor nearby, Benjamin began delving hurriedly into the pile. Yanking things out as quickly – but also as quietly – as he could, Benjamin began to form a new pile by lobbing things onto it. In his haste, one small paper bag missed the pile and landed on the floor with a crack. Moments later a yellow goo was oozing from it, together with a foul smell. Rotten eggs!

Hoping that Mops hadn't been daft enough to pack eggs amongst her collection too, Benjamin scrunched up his nose and burrowed deeper into the pile. His fingers touched soft materials. They caught on rough, scratchy things. And then they landed on a small, smooth round object. The round object was attached to a short metal bar. And, at the other end of the bar was...another small, smooth round object. Wheels! The wheels on a wheely-box! Heaving with all his might, Benjamin pulled it out. He'd found it!

What was more, it was still mighty heavy – which meant Mops's food collection must still be inside. All he had to do now was get some out, race round to lob it over the fence, then come back to set out on the return climb to the safety of their cage-block. Benjamin's mouth was already watering at the thought of what would happen after that. What a feast they were going to have!

Quickly, Benjamin trundled the wheely-box closer to the store-cave entrance. That will save time when I come back again, he thought. Then he ducked outside and hung the lantern back on its hook, satisfied that it would still cast enough light for him to unpack by.

Benjamin flipped open the lid of Mops's wheely-box. One thousand four hundred and ninety-one, clicked the count in his head.

Oh.

Or should that have been one thousand nine hundred and forty-one?

Suddenly Benjamin wasn't sure. But, he told himself, there's nothing to worry about. If Mops and Spike, hiding in the shadows of the runaround-yard, had counted up to one thousand nine hundred, they would have given him a whistle. And as he hadn't heard a whistle it meant he had plenty of time before Inspector Dictatum was due back.

So you can imagine that, as Benjamin began to unload the treasures buried in Mops's wheely-box, it came as a very nasty surprise to him to hear in quick succession a chuff and a puff and a hiss and a growl and, finally, Inspector Dictatum's terrifying roar.

An even nastier surprise was that it sounded as though Inspector Dictatum was loping rapidly towards the store-cave's entrance with every intention of coming right inside.

It sounded like that for a very good reason.

Because he was.

HUNGRY!

Inspector Dictatum's snout had begun twitching some distance away from the store-cave as an unpleasant, sap-like smell drifted towards him on the night air. It had twitched still further as the smell had grown more powerful. By the time he'd drawn close enough to be certain that the foul smell was coming from the store-cave ahead of him, Inspector Dictatum's suspicions had been well and truly raised: hence his chuff-puff-hiss-growl-terrifying roar.

Racing angrily up to the store-cave's entrance, Inspector Dictatum didn't hesitate. Something foul-smelling and suspicious was inside and it was going to live to regret it. Claws aimed like daggers, the great bear snatched the lantern from its hook and burst through the small opening with a howl of fury – only to stop suddenly, his mean eyes glittering as he glared down at the cause of all the trouble.

Slowly, Inspector Dictatum bared his ferociously sharp teeth. He was...smiling.

He lowered his lantern and scraped at the yellow

mess on the ground. He held it to his snout, quickly wrinkling it in disgust. A rotten egg! The one thing in nature that smelled like a sap, only worse.

Inspector Dictatum's smile faded. He looked round the cave. It needed sorting out, before more of his incompetent guards came trampling in, throwing things around and breaking confusingly smelly rotten eggs. But for now, it wasn't worth worrying about. The detour had put him behind schedule and Inspector Dictatum did so hate being behind schedule in terrifying the inhabitants of the Howling-Tower.

And so, pausing only to kick aside a silly sparkly-wheeled case that had been carelessly dumped near the store-cave entrance, he stomped out.

It was quite some time before Benjamin Wildfire, in his hiding place deep beneath the not-very-cobwebby pile of belongings, felt able to breathe freely again. He'd frantically burrowed his way to the bottom of the pile the moment he'd realised Inspector Dictatum was on the way. There he'd lain, motionless, while the great bear had done whatever he'd done. And there he'd stayed until he was certain the great bear had started his next lap of the tower complex and he was safe for another count of two thousand two hundred and twelve. Only then did Benjamin finally emerge.

Quickly he flipped open the top of Mops's wheely-box and stuffed as much food as he could inside his shirt.

Then, arms loaded with still more, he scurried out of the store-cave, round past the decorative cartwheel, past the end wall of the cage-block and up to the runaround-yard fence. He was greeted by two figures slithering out from beneath their sap-flap with cries of relief.

'Benjamin Wildfire!' hissed Mops, racing to the fence. 'You're alive! Oh, you're alive!'

Spike looked equally amazed. 'We thought you were done for, matey. We heard Inspector Dictatum come back and...'

He stopped and glanced guiltily at Mops. She'd already hung her head in shame and was scuffing circles on the floor with the toe of her shoe.

'Sorry,' they both said together.

'Save it for later,' said Benjamin sharply. 'Now catch this lot.'

Item by item, Benjamin lobbed the things he'd recovered over the fence. Leaving Mops and Spike to carry it all back to their cages, Benjamin began his return journey.

This went without a hitch and it seemed only moments before Benjamin was making the final exhilarating dash across the runaround-yard and diving beneath his jammed-open sap-flap to safety.

Only then did he snap, 'What happened to my warning whistle? Mops, you told me you could count as high as two thousand!'

'I can!'

'Don't tell me,' sighed Benjamin, 'you lost count!'

'I did not lose count!' said Mops, indignantly.

'So why didn't I get a warning whistle?' demanded Benjamin.

Mops pointed an irritated finger at Spike. 'Because Mister Drippy here didn't think to mention that he can't whistle.'

'Only because I thought marvel-Mops here would be able to do it!' Spike retorted angrily. 'She can do everything else – according to her.'

'Well I can't,' said Mops, biting her lip. She looked at Benjamin. 'I'm sorry.'

Spike gave Benjamin a rueful smile. 'Me too, matey.'

Benjamin looked at his two friends – and grinned. Then he laughed. And he didn't stop laughing till they'd completely unloaded all the supplies he'd brought back and shared them out equally. Then, while they ate and drank until they were hungry no more, Benjamin told Mops and Spike all about the store-cave and what it contained.

'You hid my wheely-box carefully, did you?' said Mops.

Benjamin swallowed his last mouthful, burped, and nodded. 'Yes. Just inside the entrance.'

'Good,' said Mops. 'You want to be able to find it quickly when you go back again.'

'Go back again?' cried Spike. 'After tonight? You're mad!'

'No, she's not, Spike,' said Benjamin. He pointed at what was left of the supplies he'd brought from the store-cave. 'Even if we go carefully, we've only got enough food to last us a little while longer. Then I'll have to go back to get some more.'

Spike couldn't help but agree. 'But you've got to promise me one thing before you do,' he said.

'What's that?'

'You'll teach me to whistle.'

'I promise!' laughed Benjamin.

Mops brushed the biscuit crumbs from her tattered pink clothes. 'Well, if you're in a promising mood, Benjamin Wildfire, you can make me one as well.'

'What's that, Mops?' asked Benjamin.

'Next time you won't forget to bring back my nail file!'

GRATEFUL

For Benjamin, Mops and Spike the next few days were as happy as any days spent in the Howling-Tower could possibly hope to be. That is, they were awful but not hungrily, starvingly awful.

After their feast on the night of Benjamin's expedition, the three friends were still so full that their next session in the formulations-cavern posed them no problems at all. They were easily able to ignore the brimming bowls of fatting-potion, knowing that back in their cages another tasty feast awaited them.

The only bad thing about this was that it gave them time to look around and see the full horror of what else was going on in the formulations-cavern. For instance, they saw why Yelp, the boy in the cage next door, now had an even blotchier face than before. He was having stuff rubbed into it under a sign which read (said Mops) 'wrinkle-stop snout-lotion'. Lewis, the boy who'd always had a runny nose, now had runny eyes as well. He sat, alone and shivering, in an ice-filled cubicle marked 'cure-cold'. And above it all, from the start of the day till its end, were the regular howls of pain. Benjamin resolved, there and then, to persuade Mops and Spike to pass just a little of their supplies through the bars and along to the other cages that night, so as to give everybody a little hope.

Mops and Spike agreed, although as Spike rightly pointed out, 'But only a little, matey. They're not on mouth-zero-in. We are.'

So this they did, to cries of joy instead of pain. Benjamin also, in the intervals when Inspector Dictatum's rounds had taken the great bear far enough away, taught Spike to whistle. Soon he was able to create such a shriek that everybody else in the cage-block gave him a round of applause. Everybody except Mops. She was using her hands to cover her ears.

'Yes, yes, yes!' she shouted. 'So you can whistle. Wonderful! Now give it a rest.'

Spike grinned. 'All right, no need to get in a mood just because you can't do it.'

It was true. Mops had tried but the only thing to emerge from her puckered lips was a faint humming sound (and a couple of crumbs from the last loaf-crusty). She'd had to admit that Spike's new skill was crucial, though. What with feeding themselves and now passing treats along the corridor, Benjamin's haul of supplies had almost gone. He was going to have to creep out on another store-cave raid.

He did so the very next night. This time the whole

business couldn't have worked more smoothly. Reaching the store-cave, Benjamin quickly unloaded more supplies from the wheely-box, then ran round to lob them over the runaround-yard fence to Mops and Spike. All this was managed so quickly that Benjamin had time to check some of the other bags in the store-cave before Spike's restrained warning whistle called him back.

In the formulations-cavern next morning, there was much scratching of heads. Clericus, left in charge by Doctor Calcupod, was particularly concerned.

'Numbers-these right-not,' he muttered as Benjamin, Mops and Spike were loaded onto the weighing machine one after the other. 'Saps-starving should be heavy-less.'

Lectern peered over the top of his purple scratch-pad. 'So up-make some numbers-better.'

'Up-make?' cried a shocked Clericus. 'Not can-you that-do!'

Lectern shrugged. 'See-me not-why. Me-to numbers-all same-look.'

'Which why-is pad-*you*-hold and pad-*me*-scratch,' sniffed Clericus, then faithfully recorded the figures the Quantity-Counting Assistants had called out.

So the three friends survived yet another day in the formulations-cavern. That night though, as they were marched back, Benjamin told Mops and Spike the dismal news: Mops's wheely-box was down to only a quarter full.

The moment they were pushed back into their cages, Spike asked, 'What are we going to do?'

Benjamin had the answer. 'There's my bag and lots of other bags in the store-cave,' he said. 'I've checked a few and they've got food in too. Some of it looked a bit on the old side...'

'Better to be poisoned by what you know than by fatting-potions you don't know,' said Spike solemnly.

So the next time Benjamin went hunting for food he plundered other bags. Quickly following his route (he was very good at it by now) he raced into the store-cave. Any bag that felt as if it might contain food was rapidly unloaded. Once he'd gathered up as many supplies as he could carry, Benjamin dashed round and lobbed them over the runaround-yard fence.

The system worked beautifully. Everybody knew that it was Benjamin, Mops and Spike who came first, because only they were mouth-zero-iners. But Benjamin always made sure that some food was passed out through the front bars and along the corridor. In those few moments sore eyes, streaming noses and blotchy faces were forgotten, even though the food Benjamin found in the old and dusty bags sometimes tasted old and dusty itself. At other times, especially when the food had been carefully packed, it tasted as though its original owner had prepared it only hours before.

Benjamin, Mops and Spike always remembered to give thanks to the unknown human whose supplies they were plundering. Benjamin had invented what he called a Grateful-before-meals for its very purpose.

'For what we are about to eat,' he would say quietly, 'may we be truly grateful to the boy or girl whose food this once was.'

'Absolutely,' Mops would add.

'True enough, matey,' was Spike's regular reply.

'We agree,' they would hear echoing up and down the corridor outside.

'May we meet them one sun-come in Hide-Park, where humans run free.'

Then they would tuck in, trying hard not to think that those who'd packed what they were eating almost certainly *wouldn't* be meeting them in Hide-Park; that they'd almost certainly ended their moons in the Howling-Tower, lonely and forgotten victims of Inspector Dictatum's wicked experiments.

'How long can we go on like this, do you think?' Mops said some nights later.

'For as long as we keep on finding decent food to eat in the store-cave,' said Benjamin sensibly. 'There are still plenty of bags I haven't touched.' Each one belonging to forgotten humans, he thought sadly. Humans like Duncan and Alicia Wildfire, his parents. Had they been carrying bags of supplies? Were those bags gathering dust and cobwebs in store-cave mounds somewhere?

'It'll all run out in the end,' said Spike gloomily. 'Then what?'

'Then,' said Mops, 'you'll finally have something to be miserable about. Until then, do cheer up!'

Benjamin laughed, but he knew that Spike had a point. He'd told them that on his last expedition he'd tried to reach the neighbouring block's store-cave. But it had been too far, and his fear of not hearing Spike's warning whistle had forced him to abandon the attempt. What he *hadn't* told them, though, was that he'd now got to the bottom of the fairly-cobwebby pile in their own store-cave. Next time he was going to have to start on the really-cobwebby pile, where the bags and packages looked as if they'd been in the store-cave longest of all. Any food in that pile would surely have turned green and mouldy by now.

Little did Benjamin Wildfire know that he would never find that out. For equally little did he know that his nights in the Howling-Tower (and those of Mops and Spike, too) were numbered.

Numbered by such a small number, in fact, that even Lectern could have coped with it.

To be precise – the number one.

That's how many nights they had left.

THE CRAMMING-PROCESS

Sun-come arrived with Benjamin, Mops and Spike still feeling reasonably wellfed. The sap-flap was winched high. The three friends crawled slowly out into the runaround-yard. In spite of everything they were growing weaker. Like everybody else in the cage-block, Benjamin did nothing more than sit dully on the ground. Outside the fence he saw the two powerful guard-bears marching in step, heading in the opposite direction to wherever they went at the end of sun-go runaround time. When Benjamin, Mops and Spike returned to their cage, nothing had changed. The 'Mouth-Zero-In' signs were still in place. Their food bowl was still empty.

Twelve arrived to clean their corridor. Apart from seeming to take even more care than usual as he swept the patch outside their cage, the trusty-sap did his job as thoroughly as always.

So far, so normal. It was only after Benjamin, Mops and Spike began their march to the formulations-cavern that things began to change. For a start, they were being marched much more briskly than usual, as quickly as on their first morning in the formulations-cavern, when Inspector Dictatum had been waiting to look them over with his glinting eyes.

That should have been the first clue that something was up. And when they were shoved through the cavern door, it was indeed to come face-to-snout with the great bear. Grouped around him, the Quantity-Counting Assistants stood quivering nervously. So, too, were Clericus and Lectern. Even the usually calm Doctor Calcupod had a fixed and glassy smile on her face.

'Me-let clear-be,' Inspector Dictatum growled at once. 'Saps-these have eaten-never their fatting-potions?'

'No, Sir,' said the QCAs in unison.

Inspector Dictatum scanned the figures in the shaking Lectern's purple scratch-pad. His eyes narrowed dangerously as he saw the sea of zeroes.

'Not full-mouth-one?'

'No, Sir.'

'So come-how…' said the great bear, now turning to a cowering Clericus, as he tapped one evil, curved claw on the pages of the purple pad, 'record-you-also change-none in their heavy-count? Numbers-these must wrong-be!'

'Y-yes, Inspector. N-no, Inspector,' stammered Clericus, not daring to say that he'd thought the numbers didn't add up himself.

'No? Yes? Cannot both-be!'

Doctor Calcupod gave a polite little snort. 'Inspector Dictatum, statistics can look-sometimes-so to the eye-untrained. Probably need-them just a fiddle-quick...'

'No!' roared the great bear. Thrusting out one huge paw he caught Benjamin Wildfire by the neck and dragged him forward. 'Heavy-count him now!'

Trembling, Benjamin was heaved into the weighing seat. Stones and pebbles were added until the seat had stopped swinging up and down. Checking the purple scratch-pad, then peering at the dial above the seat, Inspector Dictatum announced the result for himself.

'Same-exactly as experiment-start,' he growled in a voice that dripped with suspicion.

Mops went into the weighing seat next. 'Girl-sap also,' announced the Inspector. 'Not a pebble-difference!'

Last, in went Spike. As the weighing pointer stopped quivering, Clericus couldn't contain his cry of glee. 'Heavier-one, Sir!'

Inspector Dictatum's eyes almost popped out of his furry brown head with fury. 'Heavier-one? Nothing-him-swallow since experiment-start! Should-him be lighter-one! If sideways-him-turned, should invisible him-be!'

Dragged from the weighing pouch, Spike hurried across to join Benjamin and Mops in a fearful huddle. For the moment, though, Inspector Dictatum was devoting all his fearsome attention to Doctor Calcupod and her quivering staff.

'Thing-some here-is on-going,' he said menacingly. 'Saps-these are food-getting.'

'Not us-from,' replied Doctor Calcupod firmly. 'Nor guards-from. Saps-these are mouth-zero-in.'

'Well food-them-getting from where-some!' roared Inspector Dictatum. Then he said quietly, which made it sound even scarier: 'Listen-good. Offer-you fatting-potion to saps-these time-once-more. If some-they-eat, good-and-well. But if not-they-do, then sun-come-next use-you the Cramming-Process. Recite-you process-this.'

Immediately the QCAs began to chant:

'Saps-these will to Cramming-Chamber taken-be.

'Saps-these will chained-be on feeding-bench by foot-and-hand.

'Saps-these will encouraged-be to mouth-open by nose-pinching.

'Saps-these will inserted-have mouth-funnel of size-suitable.

'Saps-these will potion-receive by in-tipping through mouth-funnel until crammed-them-full.'

Gathering full power into their lungs, the QCAs let rip with their final rousing statement: 'Process-this flouts-not sap-rights! Process-this bearkind-benefits!'

Shaken to the core Benjamin, Mops and Spike were taken to their cubicles for what they now knew was going to be the last time. As instructed, the QCAs brought them their usual brimming bowls of fatting-potion, then stepped back to watch what happened.

'What are we going to do?' whispered Mops.

'Only thing we can do,' answered Spike. He stretched a hand towards his bowl. 'Down the lot and have done with it.'

'No!' shouted Benjamin.

'Why not, matey? A couple of good mouthfuls should be enough. Get it down, blow up like a balloon and – pop! All over.'

'No more worries,' said Mops weakly. She, too, was reaching out a hand towards her bowl. 'I think you're right, Spike.'

Around them the QCAs shuffled closer, their scratch-pads at the ready.

'No, no, no!' yelled Benjamin at the top of his voice.

His friends both paused, but neither pulled their hands back from their bowls. 'Give us one good reason why not,' said Mops.

'Because,' Benjamin said, the words tumbling out, 'I've worked out how we can all escape from the Howling-Tower! Every single sap in our cage-block!'

Spike and Mops looked at each other. Now, slowly, they *did* draw their hands back. They sat up straighter. Their faces took on looks of determination.

'That *is* a good reason,' said Spike.

'The best,' agreed Mops.

The presence of the frustrated, ready-to-swipe-them

QCAs stopped them asking Benjamin for more details. He sighed with relief. It had worked. His friends weren't going to end it all. They would hold out until that sun-go, at least.

Then, and only then, would he tell them the truth. He *hadn't* worked out how they could all escape from the Howling-Tower.

Well, not completely. He'd sort of worked out how everybody *might* be able to get out of their cage-block – but not how they would then go about escaping from the Howling-Tower itself.

No, even that wasn't quite true.

The saddest part about his plan was that one of them wouldn't even get that far. He (or she) was probably going to end up being torn to shreds by Inspector Dictatum first.

TWELVE'S CONFESSION

They did hold out until the end of the day. But as they trudged away from the formulations-cavern for the final time Benjamin, Mops and Spike were in no doubt about the fate awaiting them next sun-come. Before leaving they'd been weighed by the Quantity-Counting Assistants as usual. But this time, after Clericus had recorded their weights, Doctor Calcupod had taken the scratch-pad from Lectern's clasp and stamped a single hyphenated word on its purple cover.

'Cramming-Process,' Mops had confirmed tearfully.

The moment they were back in their cage-block, Spike came straight to the point. 'What's this plan, then?'

Benjamin braced himself to tell them the truth – but, before he could, there came a furtive, shuffling sound from out in the corridor. It was Twelve and, like Spike, he came straight to the point.

'You've been in that store-cave, haven't you?' he hissed at Benjamin.

'I—'

'Don't deny it. You've been passing food to each other

through the bars. I found the crumbs when I was sweeping this morning...'

So that's why Twelve had taken longer than usual cleaning their corridor, realised Benjamin. He didn't know what to say. So, he said nothing – at least not until he heard what Twelve said next.

'You've been jamming open the sap-flap, haven't you? Getting out when Inspector Dictatum's gone by, climbing up that tree in the runaround-yard, getting across to the roof, coming down to the sap-flap control wheel, grabbing food from the store-cave then coming back again. Right?'

'H-how did you know?' stammered Benjamin, breaking his silence.

'I didn't,' said Twelve. 'I just guessed you'd think of the same way of getting out that your...your...father did.'

Benjamin's heart leapt. 'My father? Duncan Wildfire?'

'The bravest sap I ever knew,' nodded Twelve slowly.

Spike growled suspiciously. 'I remember you saying you didn't know any Duncan Wildfire. Just like you didn't know any Alicia Wildfire, till Benjamin was nearly sold at the market and you was reminded of her.'

The trusty-sap glanced anxiously towards the corridor door. 'There's no time for explanations! I shouldn't be here at all!'

He leant through the bars of Benjamin's cage to clutch him by the arm. 'I did know your father. And your mother,' added Twelve with a gulp. 'They ran away after you were sold and vowed to find you. But they ended up here.'

'And escaped again?'

'Don't interrupt!' hissed Twelve. 'Just tell me — are you planning to make an escape bid?'

'Yes,' said Benjamin, even though he didn't know how.

'We don't have any choice,' whimpered Mops. 'They're putting us on the Cramming-Process tomorrow.'

'Poison or big bang, one way or the other we're done for,' said Spike. He gave a resigned laugh. 'I bet that's what the "D" means — "Done for". Y'know, the way this place is supposed to be the Department for Sap Training, Education and Deployment, except that the "T" really stands for "Trading" and the "E" really stands for "Experimentation".' He turned to Twelve. 'Am I right?'

'No,' said Twelve bleakly. 'It's "D" for "Disposal". In the Mincer.'

'Do not say that word!' screeched Mops.

Benjamin gasped in horror. 'You mean it really exists? That's where we'll end up?'

'Turned into sap-sages,' said Spike. 'Told you.'

'Formulations and Food,' said Twelve. 'That's how Inspector Dictatum makes most of the money.'

An awful, terrible thought had just occurred to Benjamin. It was all he could do to voice it. 'My father and mother. Did they...were they...'

'Minced? No, they were not!' said Twelve. His previous urgency was back. 'Your mother was sold, remember, and your father escaped. The only human ever to manage it – because I helped him!'

'You?'

'Yes. Now, listen. I'll tell you what I told him. There's a gate. It's past the formulations-cavern, at the end of a cobbled pathway. It's never locked. The guard-bears use it to sneak in when they stay out too late. Get out that way and you'll be close to Shadewell-Wood and the Winding-River.'

Benjamin seized the trusty-sap's hand through their cage bars in gratitude. 'Thank you, Twelve. Thank you.'

'Why's he telling us this now?' asked Mops, suspiciously.

'I bet he wants to come with us,' said Spike.

Twelve shook his head. 'No, I don't. It's too late for that now. I just want to make up for – for…'

He didn't finish. Clutching a hand to his lips, Twelve turned and scurried away, down the corridor and through the door at the end.

Behind him, Benjamin's heart was singing at what the trusty-sap had just revealed. His parents had both left the Howling-Tower alive. What was more, they now knew of a way out of the awful place. Twelve had even confirmed something that Benjamin had wondered about but hadn't known for sure.

'Did you hear what he said when he was describing

the route I'd taken to the store-cave? The *sap-flap control wheel!*'

'Is that good?' asked Mops.

'Yes!' said Benjamin. 'It means those big wheels aren't decorations at all. They control the opening and closing of the sap-flaps!'

It all made sense. The network of chains leading from the cage-block roof across the dome-shaped roof and down to the wheel; the two powerful guard-bears marching *towards* that wheel before the sap-flaps came down at sun-go and *away* from it after they'd risen at sun-come. Their job simply had to be turning that huge control wheel to raise and lower the sap-flaps.

'That's important, is it?' asked Spike, drawing as near to Benjamin's cage as he could. 'Important to your plan to get us out of here?'

'Vitally important, Spike,' said Benjamin.

'Well I hope it don't include us having to turn that wheel. If it takes the strength of them two guard-bears then we'll have no chance.'

'It doesn't,' smiled Benjamin.

Mops squeezed close on Benjamin's other side. 'Well, don't keep it to yourself. I'm almost bursting! What *is* this plan?'

So Benjamin told them. He explained where each of them would have to go, what they would have to do when they got there, and why they had to do it if the plan was going to work.

'Wondrous,' said Mops when he'd finished.

'Challenging, matey,' said Spike, 'but nothing we can't handle.'

'You like it, then?' asked Benjamin.

'I do indeed,' said Mops. 'I'm all in favour.'

'Me an' all,' said Spike. 'Let's give it a go.'

'In spite of the *one* little detail I'm not so keen on,' said Mops.

'Is that the same little detail I'm thinking of, Squawker?' said Spike.

'That either you, me or Benjamin is highly likely to get caught by Inspector Dictatum and ripped to shreds?' asked Mops.

'That's the one,' said Spike.

Benjamin hugged them both. His friends had seen the awful danger in his plan and were still prepared to go ahead with it. Now there was nothing more he could say or do except to wait for the sound of grinding chains to announce that their sap-flaps were about to rise for their last runaround time ever.

FLIGHT FOR FREEDOM

They didn't stay outside for long. They'd decided against telling the others in their cage-block about the plan in case it all went horribly wrong.

'Better not to raise their hopes at all,' Benjamin had said.

So even before the two powerful guard-bears began their march towards the sap-flap control wheel they were back in their cages, rock at the ready. As the sap-flap began to descend, Benjamin held the rock in position. The trick worked as successfully as ever.

Nervously, they waited for Inspector Dictatum to begin his rounds. Bang on time, the powerful bear emerged to chuff and puff and hiss and growl and, just before he disappeared from view, let rip with his opening roar of the night. Knowing what was ahead, Benjamin, Mops and Spike were more terrified by that roar than they'd even been before.

Even so, the moment Inspector Dictatum moved away, the three friends slid quickly out under their sap-flap. Swiftly they hurried across the runaround-yard.

This time, however, it wasn't Benjamin who leapt on to the fence. It was Spike. The plan had begun in earnest.

Nothing like as nimble as Benjamin, Spike took far longer to clamber up the swaying fence and swing himself across to the lowest branch. When finally he did reach it, the branch sagged horribly.

Spike gave a low moan, 'It's going to break!'

'Oh, stop whining and help me up!' hissed Mops.

Straddling the thickest part of the branch, Spike reached down with both large hands. On the ground, Benjamin cupped his own hands together so that Mops could slide one dainty foot between them. Then he launched her up so that Spike could grab her hands and pull her up beside him.

'This branch is going to break!' moaned Mops the moment she was there.

'Now *you* stop whining!' hissed Benjamin. 'And get a move on, you don't have long.'

According to the plan, Benjamin was the one who had to keep count this time – and he'd already reached eight hundred and seventy-five. Anxiously, he gazed up into the tree.

Spike had reached the higher branch. He was picking his way uncertainly along it. Following behind, Mops was copying him exactly.

Before he knew it, Benjamin was counting silently: one thousand nine hundred and twenty, one thousand nine hundred and twenty-one...

They were nearly there! Spike had swung himself off the end of the higher branch and down onto the flat top of the dome-shaped roof. He was helping Mops down. Now they were falling flat on their faces, so that they couldn't be seen (or smelled) by a prowling bear below.

One thousand nine hundred and ninety-nine, two thousand, two thousand and one...

Benjamin gave a low whistle. Spike and Mops looked across and put their thumbs in the air. And, moments later, Inspector Dictatum lumbered round the side of the store-cave without being any the wiser that its roof was occupied.

Benjamin waited until the great bear appeared beyond the fence. This next step of the plan was down to him. Leaping out from behind the tree, Benjamin waved his arms and jumped up and down so wildly that even a bear with blinkers couldn't have missed him.

'I'm free!' he screamed. 'I'm free, FREE! Free as a Hide-Park human!'

He sang. He danced. Benjamin did everything he could think of to leave the Inspector in no doubt as to how joyfully happy he was at being loose in the runaround-yard when he wasn't supposed to be.

That was the plan. It seemed to be working, too. Inspector Dictatum's face had taken on a frown of total mystification. Just as Benjamin had hoped, the bear's slow brain appeared to be struggling to work out how a sap could be outside at a time when saps were supposed to be securely locked inside. It was time to make that clear — for if he was watching Benjamin, then he wouldn't be turning his attention anywhere else.

Still whooping with delight, Benjamin raced back across the runaround-yard and dived beneath his jammed-open sap-flap. Dancing a couple of loud laps round his cage, he then raced back out into the runaround-yard once more and straight up to the fence.

A light seemed to come on behind Inspector Dictatum's black eyes. 'If a sap can be outside, then vanish inside, then be outside again,' it suggested the vicious bear was thinking, 'then that sap's sap-flap must be open!' It was too gloomy for him to see whether that was so, but it had to be the only possible explanation.

That's what Benjamin hoped it suggested, anyway. Placing two fingers on his tongue, he now let rip with a piercing whistle. It was the signal Spike and Mops had been waiting for. While Benjamin had been keeping Inspector Dictatum occupied with his antics, they'd been scrambling down from the dome-shaped roof to land beside the sap-flap control wheel.

'Inspector Dic-ta-tum!' screeched Mops.

And Spike hollered, 'Come round here, you ugly brute!'

Inspector Dictatum swung round in the direction of their voices. His black eyes flashed in anger. An unexplained sap in the runaround-yard was bad. But a sap *outside* the runaround-yard was so bad that there wasn't a word to describe it. Unsheathing his razor-sharp claws, the furious bear turned away from Benjamin and began to race towards the voices of Mops and Spike.

They heard the thunder of Inspector Dictatum's paw-steps even before he rounded the corner. But did they use the time to run for it? They did not. Running wasn't in Benjamin's plan – not quite yet, anyway.

First, they joined hands and gripped the great wheel with all the strength they could muster.

'Heave!' screamed Mops, pretending to tug at the sap-flap control wheel with all her might. (Yes, pretending.)

'Heave!' shouted Spike, pretending (yes, pretending) to do exactly the same.

Only when Inspector Dictatum had lumbered to within striking distance, did they let go of the sap-flap control wheel. *Then* they ran! Not in the same direction, though. Mops ran one way. Spike, with one last piercing whistle, ran the opposite way.

Inspector Dictatum slithered to a halt, totally confused. His feeble mind began adding together what he'd just seen – to come up (just as Benjamin had planned) with completely the wrong answer.

'Saps outside? Then must sap-flaps open-be. That-why saps-two control-wheel-turning! So...must-me control-wheel back-turn!'

And so, thinking all the sap-flaps were open when

only one was, Inspector Dictatum lumbered up to the control-wheel. Heaving on it with all his might he discovered (of course) that it wouldn't turn the way it usually did. Why? Once again his weak brain came up with the wrong answer. Deciding that he must simply have forgotten how to do the job (a common fault amongst inspectors), he heaved the wheel in the opposite direction instead.

Magically, wonderfully, Benjamin saw this next stage of his plan unfold before his eyes. As Inspector Dictatum turned the control-wheel, mistakenly thinking he was closing a collection of open sap-flaps, every single one of the closed sap-flaps began to clank open!

He wasted no time. 'Come out!' he screamed, racing from cage to cage. 'Come out, everybody, come out!'

'What's going on?' demanded one.

Seeing their sap-flaps inexplicably open in the middle of the night, the boys and girls did just that. Out they crawled: first one, then another, then another – until the trickle became a stream and the stream became a flood.

'Please don't let it be more experiments,' pleaded another.

'It's your chance to escape!' cried Benjamin, finally able to tell them. 'Wait here – and be ready!'

Racing back across the runaround-yard, Benjamin climbed up the fence in record time. Leaping across to the tree, he clambered quickly up to the branch which led across to the dome-shaped roof – then stopped, waiting.

Benjamin held his breath. This was it, the moment they'd known they'd have to face. If Inspector Dictatum decided to chase and shred either Mops or Spike, then it would give up time to help the others over the fence and away. But if, instead, he came for Benjamin...

Down below, Inspector Dictatum was looking completely stunned. After turning the sap-flap control wheel, the last thing he'd expected to hear was a racket so loud that it could only have been made by a swarm of saps pouring out from their cages. Exactly how this could be, he simply wasn't able to work out.

But now, as he looked up and saw Benjamin high in the branches of the runaround-yard tree, the bear's wicked eyes glinted with understanding. So *that* was how the two saps had got out of the yard! And now the hated, red-haired one was trying the same thing! Into Inspector Dictatum's mind flashed the memory that had haunted him for so long - of that other red-haired sap, Duncan Wildfire. In that instant his mind was made up. Of the three saps on the loose, *this* was the one he was going to rip to pieces first.

With a shattering roar of rage, Inspector Dictatum started to bound up the sloping store-cave wall. Within moments the great bear had clawed his way to the top of the dome-shaped roof.

Benjamin bided his time. His mind was screaming at him to move, to get away from Inspector Dictatum as fast as he possibly could. But he didn't. Instead he edged towards the great bear, closer and closer, until he was in what he hoped was just the right position. Then he began bouncing lightly up and down on his branch so that the end waggled invitingly before Inspector Dictatum's black eyes.

Those eyes glinted. The huge bear's strong back legs braced themselves. And then, with another shattering roar, Inspector Dictatum launched himself, thrusting one set of ugly yellow claws out towards Benjamin as he landed on the bouncing branch – and it snapped under his weight! Snapped at the very point where Benjamin had deliberately positioned himself, directly above the runaround-yard fence. In a shower of leaves and twigs, down plummeted Inspector Dictatum to land on top of the barbed wire. As the jagged spikes punctured his furry hide, the bear let out a mighty howl. But, for him, worse was to come. He was still falling. Flailing wildly with his free paw, Inspector Dictatum looped five yellow claws into the links of the fence, gripping it with all his might to stop himself falling any further.

It almost worked.

Inspector Dictatum did indeed stop falling – but not for very long. As with the branch, the strain of the great bear's weight proved too much for the runaround-yard fence. With a groan of twisting wire, the fence buckled and wobbled...and, finally, toppled over completely.

For a moment, the sight of the runaround-yard fence being broken down was too much for the captured boys and girls to take in. They simply stood, staring at the gaping hole Inspector Dictatum had ripped in it – until Benjamin's scream cut through their confusion.

'Run! Run as fast as you can!'

Startled into action, they began moving. To Benjamin's delight it was Yelp, the blotchy-faced boy, who reacted first. With a shout of joy he ran forward, cleverly avoiding the barbed wire on the ground by jumping onto Inspector Dictatum then off again.

'I'm free!' he screamed. 'I'm free!'

The others began to flood after him now – and Inspector Dictatum was powerless to stop them. His mighty paw was still entangled in the fence. The last to go was Brunhilde, the tearful girl from the cage-cart. Having seen all the others do it, she finally plucked up enough courage to follow them.

'Thank you, Benjamin Wildfire!' she cried.

'May we meet again in Hide-Park!' shouted Benjamin, as Brunhilde ran after the others and vanished into the darkness.

And then, in the deathly silence that followed, Benjamin Wildfire closed his eyes and awaited his fate.

There was little else he *could* do. For when Inspector Dictatum had leapt from the store-cave roof and thrust out one set of ugly claws towards Benjamin he had, in fact, reached him. Those claws had looped into the waistband of Benjamin's trousers and stuck so fast that when Inspector Dictatum had fallen, Benjamin had been dragged down with him. It was Inspector Dictatum's other paw that had flailed wildly, become entangled in the runaround-yard fence and pulled it down. Try as he might as the others escaped, Benjamin simply hadn't been able to break free. Inspector Dictatum hadn't given him a chance. Down in the deepest parts of that large bear's small brain a voice had been shouting: 'Revenge! Revenge-me-have on the trouble-cause!'

Benjamin now found himself being lifted upwards, until he was level with Inspector Dictatum's black eyes and could smell the foul breath wafting across his evil yellow teeth. He closed his eyes, waiting for the first fierce claw to land on him. But instead he heard, in a deep growl that dripped pure hatred: 'Wildfire, suffer-you-will as sap-none before-suffered. Going-you-are to the Mincer — but stunned-not with head-wallop. Going-you-are awake-wide.'

SAP-PREPARATION

Benjamin wasn't dealt with immediately. After Inspector Dictatum had finally managed to work his claws free of the fence – and it wasn't easy – he then set about covering things up so that no blame could possibly fall on him.

He went back to the sap-flap control wheel. This time he closed the flaps, so that only that of Benjamin's remained open, still jammed by the round rock.

Then he heaved up the big branch that he'd snapped off and laid it across the crumpled fence so that it looked for all Bear Kingdom as if it had caused the damage rather than him.

Only then did he raise the alarm and haul the sleeping guard-bears from their quarters.

The bleary-eyed guards were despatched to all corners of the Howling-Tower to search for the escaped saps. This they did dutifully, none of them being either brave or stupid enough to mention the little gate they always left open for emergencies.

Then Doctor Calcupod was summoned. She arrived,

yawning. Behind her trotted Clericus. Behind him came Lectern. For a moment, Benjamin thought that, for once, the dumpy bear wasn't carrying a scratch-pad. But he was. The reason he hadn't seen it straight away was because this pad's cover was as black as the night.

Now they began to deal with Benjamin. Flanked by four torch-carrying guard-bears he was thrust forward, away from the cage-block. Past the formulations-cavern he was marched. Then past the cobbled alleyway Twelve had told them about – and along which, he prayed, Mops and Spike had led the others long since. On further, until he saw ahead the ghostly white outline of the Howling-Tower's thick rear walls.

Along the ramparts a group of torches flickered brightly above an ornate arch. Beneath this arch, at its far end, stood a blackened grille gate. Benjamin could see through it for only a short distance before the track was swallowed by the darkness. He had no doubts what lay beyond that gate, though. The Mincer.

'Dead-stop!' Inspector Dictatum's command echoed around the walls and ceiling of the archway.

Benjamin Wildfire was halted. Built into one side of the archway was a solid door. A guard-bear unlocked this door and stood to attention beside it.

'The formalities-usual, Doctor Calcupod,' growled Inspector Dictatum. 'And short-keep it.'

Doctor Calcupod inclined her head ever so slightly

towards a guard-bear. In one violent action the guard-bear ripped the shirt from Benjamin's back.

'Full-care!' roared Inspector Dictatum. 'Injure-you sap-this and will-you Mincer-go with-him! Want-me-him enough-fit to all agony-feel.'

Doctor Calcupod bent to inspect the number at the top of Benjamin's arm. 'Sap-number: one four three seven two. Name-known?'

Lectern solemnly opened his black scratch-pad – the same scratch-pad, Benjamin now realised, as the one he'd seen him holding on that first night he'd been brought to the Howling-Tower. Clericus leafed back through the heavy pages.

'Benjamin Wildfire,' he said, finding his entry from that night.

Doctor Calcupod's eyes flickered in recognition. 'As-in Duncan Wildfire, Inspector?' she asked. 'Knew-me memory-mine was very names-good! Duncan Wildfire – the only-and-one sap-escapee. Correct?'

Inspector Dictatum muttered something inaudible and (had anybody been able to hear it) unpleasant.

'Now name-what his lady-sap?' Doctor Calcupod rubbed the bridge of her snout with an elegant claw. 'Alicia! Right-me?'

Inspector Dictatum was growing seriously impatient. 'Right-you!' he said with a snarl. 'Now-happy?'

Doctor Calcupod smiled. She was looking forward to the future. This was a catastrophe of the highest order.

If she wasn't very much mistaken, Inspector Dictatum would soon be inspected himself. And when he was, her stock of ledgers were going to prove very valuable indeed. Until then, she might as well humour the bossy great oaf and get on with his unpleasant plans.

'Begin Sap-sage Preparation-Process,' she said. 'Step-first: thorough-wash.'

Benjamin's shirt had already been ripped from his back, of course. Now the same guard-bear tore (rather more carefully, remembering Inspector Dictatum's warning) the rest of Benjamin's clothes away. They were tossed in the corner.

This done, the other guard-bears hurled buckets of ice-cold water over Benjamin's head. Rough lumps of sponge were pounded against his skin, after which he was rubbed dry with lumps of straw.

'Step-second,' said Doctor Calcupod, 'flavour-coat.'

Benjamin was now draped in a large, crimson garment. It covered him with room to spare. It stretched down to the ground and had a large hood which flopped so far forwards that his head almost disappeared inside. But for all its size, the garment didn't seem to be made for warmth. It was wafer-thin and smelled of honey and wild berries. That's when Doctor Calcupod's command sank in: *flavour-coat*. He would be wearing this garment when he went to the Mincer!

'Step-third: soak-leave…'

'Until sun-come!' snarled Inspector Dictatum, ending the recipe with a touch of his own.

And with that, Benjamin was thrust through the door in the archway wall. His final night in the Howling-Tower was to be spent in the condemned-cellar.

THE CONDEMNED-CELLAR

The condemned-cellar was tiny. A short flight of stairs led down from the door. At the bottom Benjamin found a stone bench he could lay on. It was covered in the same crimson material his garment was made from. So as not to spoil his taste, he assumed.

Through the tiny, barred opening high in the cellar wall he could see two lone stars twinkling in the night sky. They made him think of Mops and Spike.

Had they reached the secret gate?

Had they led the other saps from their cage-block to safety?

Would they reach Hide-Park?

What was Hide-Park like?

How would it feel to wake up every morning knowing you were free?

And, as he looked up again at those two glittering stars – were his parents there?

That's how Benjamin spent his last night in the Howling-Tower, dreaming and wondering – until the sound of the door opening at the top of the stairs told him that he never would know the answers to these questions.

'Breakfast,' said a familiar voice.

'Twelve!'

The trusty-sap was carrying a tray. On it was a heaped bowl and a steaming cup.

'What's this?' asked Benjamin.

'Condemned sap's breakfast,' said Twelve. He tried to smile, but it only came out as a strangled sob. He wiped away a tear that was trickling down his wrinkled cheek. 'I bribed the meals trusty-sap to let me bring it. Sort of – reward. For what you did.'

'You heard about it?' said Benjamin.

Twelve nodded. His eyes, normally so dull and listless, positively shone.

'Couldn't *help* hearing about it. Inspector Dictatum's been going mad all night. Non-stop meetings – with Doctor Calcupod, then the guard-bears, then the Quantity-Counting Assistants...'

'But – why?'

'To try and cover his tracks, of course. If one of those children is found by a sap-loving bear and traced back to this place he'll be in trouble. One look will be all it will take to see how badly they've been treated. Before he knows it, Inspector Dictatum will find himself being inspected.'

'You said *if* one of them is found,' said Benjamin. 'They haven't been caught then?'

'Not one. Twenty-three got out. None have come back.' Twelve smiled in admiration. 'I bet they're glad they were put in your cage-block.'

'We couldn't have done it without your help, Twelve.'

'No, but you could have just got away on your own. You didn't have to stay and help the others. That took courage, Benjamin.'

Benjamin looked up at the barred opening. The two stars were beginning to fade. The sky was getting lighter. Sun-come wasn't far away. But he was going to go to the Mincer with joy in his heart and his head held high.

'Thanks for telling me the news, Number Twelve,' he said, standing up.

Twelve put a hand on his shoulder and forced him down again.

'I haven't finished yet. Now listen and listen good. And just for once — don't argue...'

DEAREST MOPS

Now just like Benjamin Wildfire, you may have been wondering what had happened to Mops, Spike and the other twenty-one boys and girls who'd managed to escape from the runaround-yard thanks to Benjamin's bravery and quick thinking.

The answer is, that Mops and Spike had led them all to the gate Twelve had told them about. They'd dived through it (Mops remembering to close it securely after the last had done so). Almost immediately they'd found themselves in Shadewell-Wood a wood so dense that they couldn't possibly be spotted from the tower ramparts (which is why the crafty stop-out guard-bears used it, of course).

From there, twenty-two of those exultant, escaping saps had scattered. They'd gone in all directions.

Some (those who were attracted to water and could swim) raced for the Winding-River, to take refuge amongst the thick beds of reeds and rushes which grew all along its banks.

Others decided to run back into the teeming

centre of Lon-denium with its many hidey-holes under bridges and in the deep tunnels where the Under-Town slither-trains ran.

Yet more had decided to take their chances on a life in the countryside. They'd raced away from both Lon-denium and the Winding-River, aiming instead for the forest of towering trees they could see in the far, far distance. Perhaps (they hoped) it would be a forest the bears hadn't yet reached with their cart-track building. And, even if that wasn't the case, there would surely be plenty of hiding places amongst all those trees.

Only one of the escaping saps had done something different. It had been the cause of Mops's and Spike's final, and fiercest, argument.

After plunging into the wooded area they'd ducked and dodged between the trees for no more than a short way. Then Mops had stopped running and hopped down into a shallow ditch.

'Come on, matey!' Spike had hissed, even as he'd hopped down into the ditch beside her. 'This is no time for a rest.'

'What about Benjamin?' said Mops.

'He said to run. You heard him.'

'I know he said it,' Mops had cried. 'But did he *mean* it?'

'If he hadn't meant it he wouldn't have said it!'

'But he might have meant it when he said it, then

after saying it decided he didn't mean it. But as we'd already gone, he didn't have a chance to say it!'

Spike had gnashed his teeth in frustration. 'So how are you going to find that out? Go back into the Howling-Tower and ask him?'

'Of course not...'

'Hooray,' Spike had said, getting ready to move again.

Then Mops had added, 'I shall wait for him here.'

'What!'

'I shall wait for Benjamin Wildfire here. Then, when he escapes, I can ask him if he meant what he said. And, if he did, *then* I'll run for it and leave him behind.'

'But he'll be with you!' Spike had yelled.

Mops had given a flicker of a smile. 'Silly me. So he will. In that case we'll be able to run away together again, won't we?'

'And what if Benjamin doesn't escape?' hissed Spike. 'What then?'

'Then I shall be waiting for quite a long time,' said Mops softly.

That had been the end. 'Well you'll be waiting on your own!' Spike had scrambled up to sit on the lip of the ditch. 'Benjamin said to go – and I'm going!'

'Go on, then.'

'I am.'

'What are you waiting for?'

Spike had scratched his head. Then he'd said,

'Nothing. I'm waiting for nothing. I came here on my own and now I'm going on my own.'

Mops had reached up to him then, touching him lightly on his strong arm. 'Goodbye, Spike. See you in Hide-Park.'

'Goodbye, Squawker,' Spike had replied, with a smile of unutterable sadness. 'Goodbye...Mops.'

Mops had watched him go then, leaping and plunging through the thick undergrowth until he'd disappeared from sight.

She'd cried.

Then she'd dried her eyes and settled down to wait for Benjamin Wildfire for as long as it took.

Sun-come (the same sun-come at which Number Twelve had brought Benjamin his last breakfast) crept up on Mops. Like Benjamin, she hadn't slept at all during the night. Apart from everything else, it had become terribly noisy. After a period of eerie quiet (the period during which Inspector Dictatum had been covering his tracks and the guard-bears had been guiltily searching everywhere except the area near the unlocked gate) there had followed a spell of frightening activity.

Out from the Howling-Tower had poured streams of guard-bears, mounted on torch-lit carts. Mops had shrunk down fearfully in her ditch, expecting to be discovered at any moment. But not one of the pursuing guards had bothered to leave the cart-track, clearly not expecting any of the escapees to be hiding so close to the Howling-Tower itself. On they'd trundled, their torch-lights slowly melting into the darkness.

They'd not returned until the sky in the east was taking on the brightest of orange tinges. That, together with the light cast by the now guttering torches, was enough for Mops to look into every cage-cart that trundled past.

Each time she expected to see the face of Spike peering out from between a set of bars. But she didn't. The first cage-cart was empty. So was the second. They all were! Not one of the children had been recaptured.

By the time the whole posse was back inside the tower walls, sun-come had arrived completely. Feeling safer, Mops crept out from her ditch. She wanted to get a better idea of exactly where she'd ended up.

She'd ended up (she now saw) near a cart-track which ran alongside the Winding-River, not far from where it bubbled and swirled beneath a great iron bridge. The cart-track only followed the line of the Winding-River for a short distance, though. Then it swung round to meet a black grille gate beneath an archway set into the Howling-Tower's thick white walls.

Looking hard, Mops saw that there was another track which led out from the grille gate. Forking away from it, this track led directly to the foot of a stairway. As for the stairway, that rose up towards the top of a tall, cylindrical building positioned right at the very edge of a small dock. A noise was coming from it. A metallic scrunching, spinning noise, as though the building held a lump of machinery that was churning round and round and...

The Mincer! It had to be!

And built deliberately outside the Howling-Tower's walls, so that Inspector Dictatum could always say, paw on heart, 'Sap-mincing never here-happened!'

Mops closed her eyes in horror – only to force them open again as another sound began drifting towards her. Not a spinning, crunching sound this time, but a slow, heavy drum beat.

She dragged her attention back to the grille gate. Walking slowly through it was a young cub, a round drum hanging from a silver chain round his neck. At the foot of the stairway, the drum-bear stopped but his mournful beat didn't.

Mops gasped. Coming through the gate now were two figures she'd hoped never to see again. Even from where she was, the gigantic bulk of Inspector Dictatum was unmistakable. So was the petite shape of Doctor Calcupod, with Clericus and Lectern one pace behind her. They all stopped at the foot of the stairway. Doctor Calcupod, as ever, seemed to be dictating a record of what was happening for Clericus to note in Lectern's ledger. As for what Inspector Dictatum was doing – that was very clear. With his largest, yellowest claw he was pointing up at the top of the stairway. No, not just pointing, realised Mops. Pointing – and commanding…

That's when she saw him. He'd walked slowly through the archway gate surrounded by a whole squad of guard-bears.

A shortish figure.

Uprightish, too.

And proud. With his head held high, he was approaching the bottom of the stairway with a step so firm that it could only be that of a human.

The figure was covered from head to toe in a billowing crimson garment. Inspector Dictatum appeared to be glaring at him but the human was refusing to look his way as he took his last steps.

Mops choked back a cry. What they'd done to him she couldn't bear to think, but she had no doubt who it was. The crimson-clad figure had begun to climb the stairway, proudly but slowly, as if he had aged in the short time since she and Spike had raced to their freedom.

'Oh, Benjamin Wildfire,' sighed Mops from the very bottom of her heart. 'Dear Benjamin Wildfire.'

'Yes?' said a voice.

FAREWELL

Benjamin dived down into the ditch beside Mops.

'Don't you *ever* do what you're told?' he hissed. 'You should be miles away by now!'

For the first time in her life Mops was almost lost for words. All she could manage was, 'Benjamin? Benjamin! Oh, Benjamin, Benjamin, Benjamin!'

Benjamin nodded, happy and desperately sad at the same time. 'Yes – thanks to Twelve.'

Only then did Mops realise that Benjamin wasn't wearing his usual shirt and shorts. He was wearing an orange trusty-suit. On his head, completely covering his red hair, was an orange trusty-cap.

Stunned, Mops looked back at the stairway. The crimson-clad figure was starting to climb up, two guard-bears a step behind him. The drum beats were getting faster. At the bottom of the stairway, Inspector Dictatum was clapping his paws together and swaying in time with the beats.

'Twelve? You mean...'

'Yes,' Benjamin nodded. 'He took my place. "Gladly,"
he said.'

Quickly, he told Mops about how Twelve had come to
him in the condemned-cellar; how he'd delivered his
breakfast, then begun to peel off his orange trusty-suit
and cap; and what had happened next.

'Put this on,' Twelve had said, 'and give me that
thing you're wearing.'

'But...'

'I said don't argue! I'm taking your place. Gladly.'

'But...'

'Don't argue! Benjamin, you're now going to go up
those cellar stairs carrying this tray. The guard-bears are
half asleep, they're not used to being up all night.
Besides, they won't stop you. No bear will, not if you're
wearing a trusty-suit. Go straight to the gate I told you
about. And don't dawdle, just in case Inspector
Dictatum checks under this crimson dressing and
discovers he's sending me to the Mincer instead of you.'

'But...' Benjamin had begun again, and this time he
would not stay silent, '...why? Why are you doing this
for me?'

Twelve had looked at him, then. Tenderly, as if
searching his face for a memory.

'I'm not doing it for you,' he said finally. 'I'm doing
it for your mother. To repay her.'

'My mother?'

'Alicia Wildfire. The most beautiful woman I've ever

seen. And for your father. The bravest man I've ever known.'

'Tell me about them — please!'

'We haven't time!'

'Please!' Benjamin had cried. 'I won't go until you do.'

And so Twelve had told him, hurriedly, as the two of them had exchanged clothes. About how Benjamin's parents had been brought to the Howling-Tower. About how Benjamin's father Duncan had told him, Number Twelve, about his dream of escaping and finding his long-lost son and taking him to Hide-Park.

'So he really believed in Hide-Park too,' cried Benjamin. 'It wasn't just a story he'd made up. And you helped him escape.'

Twelve smiled thinly. 'The only human ever to escape from the Howling-Tower. Until you came along.'

'Twelve, you've done enough for me and my family already. I can't let you go to the Mincer in my place.'

'You can! And when you hear the rest you'll want me to.'

He took a deep breath, as if summoning up the courage to say something he'd wanted to say for many moons.

'I helped your father escape because I wanted Alicia for myself. I loved her, you see. Inspector Dictatum hadn't begun to change things then and I was hoping she'd be trained to be a trusty-sap and spend her days with me. Anyway, I'd promised to help Alicia escape too. Your father wouldn't have left her otherwise. The arrangement was that he'd find a safe hiding place outside, then return on the next full moon. I was going to bring your mother out to the gate to meet him. Except that...I didn't.'

'What?' gasped Benjamin. 'What did you do?'

'I deliberately made a noise and attracted Inspector Dictatum's attention. Your father had no choice but to run for it. He was never seen again.'

'And my mother?' said Benjamin quietly.

Twelve hung his head. 'I was paid back. In anger, Inspector Dictatum started his Trading, Experimentation and Disposal scheme shortly after. He sent your mother to Fleeceham Market – and she didn't come back. A bear rich enough to pay any price had bought her.'

'And you've never seen her again either?'

'Oh, but I have,' sighed Twelve. 'Every night, in my dreams. I see her sobbing because of what I did.'

The trusty-sap had thrust the breakfast tray into Benjamin's hands then urged him up the steps and out of the condemned-cellar. 'Find them, Benjamin,' he'd sighed. 'Tell them I'm sorry.'

In the safety of the ditch, Mops had listened in silence to Benjamin's story. Now, as he finished, she pointed out towards the stairway leading up to the Mincer. Twelve had almost reached the top.

'You must tell them about what he did for you, too,'

she said. 'They'll surely forgive him when they hear that.'

Benjamin knew she was right. In his heart, he'd forgiven Twelve already. That's why he'd joined Mops in the ditch instead of racing away at once. He'd felt it his duty to watch Twelve's end, however hard it would be.

The trusty-sap had reached the top of the stairway. Now, he turned. Beneath him the two guard-bears watched and waited. Behind Twelve yawned a black hole which could only lead down into the Mincer. At the foot of the stairway, Inspector Dictatum's huge shoulders were wobbling. They could hear his deep, growly, mocking laughter.

Until, that is, Twelve suddenly ripped away the hood of his crimson dressing with a flourish. Then, as Inspector Dictatum saw he'd been tricked, Benjamin and Mops heard the great bear let loose a howl of rage. But even that howl was as nothing compared to the one that followed – when Twelve, instead of jumping through the black hole to meet his end in the Mincer, dived joyously from the top of the stairway to plunge headfirst into the murky waters of the dock.

'Yes!' urged Benjamin from the bottom of his heart. 'Go, Twelve, go!'

Mops clutched at her face. 'What if he can't swim? He'll drown!'

'I don't think you need worry about that, Mops. Look!'

If Twelve hadn't known how to swim when he'd dived into the dock, then he'd learned amazingly quickly. A crimson-clad shape was already ploughing a foaming furrow out of the dock, heading straight for the Winding-River and the sanctuary of the shadows beneath the iron bridge.

What was more, no bear appeared to be giving chase — even though, as all bears are very good swimmers, they'd have almost certainly caught up with Twelve quite quickly. Inspector Dictatum howled and pointed, but none of the guard-bears made a move. Inspector Dictatum's days were over, and they knew it.

So did Doctor Calcupod. She was dictating gleefully and furiously. Beside her, Clericus's writing-claw was bouncing up and down so rapidly that Lectern was having difficulty in keeping his scratch-pad balanced.

It was Mops who cut short the pleasure of the moment. Scrambling up the side of the ditch, she cried, 'Right, what are we waiting for, then?'

Pausing only to take a last look at Twelve and wish him well, Benjamin scambled up beside her. 'We?' he grinned.

'Yes, we. Now c'mon, let's go! Things to do, things to do!'

'You mean — you're coming with me, Mops? *Again*?'

'Coming with you? Of course I'm coming with you!' Mops put her hands on her hips and stared him in the face. 'Benjamin Wildfire, since meeting me you've discovered that your father's still alive and your mother's been sold to a rich bear – so she's probably alive as well!'

'And we've discovered that Hide-Park really exists, too,' said Benjamin.

'Precisely,' said Mops. 'And without me you won't find *any* of them! So, as I said – what are we waiting for?'

'Nothing, Mops,' cried Benjamin Wildfire, happily. 'Nothing at all!'

And so, without another word, the pair turned their backs on the Howling-Tower and raced off to begin their escape for real.

Well, *almost* without another word. As they plunged through the undergrowth you might just have heard Mops say: 'You didn't think of bringing any of that condemned sap's breakfast out with you I suppose? Typical...'

END OF VOLUME 1

LOOK OUT FOR THE SECOND
AND THIRD VOLUMES IN THE
BEAR KINGDOM TRILOGY

THE
FIGHTING
PIT

ISBN: 1846162149

AND

THE
HUNTING
FOREST

ISBN: 184616043X

AND TURN THE PAGE TO GET A
TASTER OF WHAT'S TO COME...

THE FIGHTING PIT

Benjamin Wildfire and Mops headed deep into Shadewell-Wood, rejoicing with every step that they were getting further and further away from the horrors of the Howling-Tower.

They travelled only at night, from sun-go until the first fingers of sun-come were feeling their way into the sky. During the light-time they kept well hidden. Dark and muddy cavities beneath the roots of fallen trees were especially useful – if not pleasant.

'Look at the state of my dress!' Mops had wailed more than once.

Her once-pretty pink outfit, which had become very dirty and bedraggled during their time caged in the Howling-Tower, was now in tatters. Shreds of material dangled down from the hem and embarassing holes revealed the pink things she had on beneath.

Benjamin's outfit had hardly any holes, but it too – just like his red hair – was now caked in mud. This was actually a good thing in his case, for the suit he was wearing had once been bright orange. It was the uniform of a Howling-Tower trusty-sap. In that accursed place a few humans had been trained to work. One of these, known to them only as Number Twelve, had bravely helped Benjamin escape by giving him his suit to wear.

Moving through Shadewell-Wood in darkness hadn't been easy. Parts were open and smooth but, in others, clutching branches and piercing thorns had slowed them to a crawl. Finally, early on the fourth night following their escape from the Howling-Tower, the wood began to thin. Through the trees they could see a torch-lit track, with a steady stream of carts trundling along it.

After a while the stream of carts slowed to a trickle. Still frightened about being spotted, Benjamin and Mops ventured slowly out from the cover of the wood. Dodging in and out of the shadows, they followed the curving line of the cart-track. It brought them to a sprawling group of dens.

Most of these dens were grey and mound-shaped, with stained slate roofs which sloped down almost to the ground. Their wide wooden doorways were dimly lit and gloomy. None showed any sign of being occupied. But on the edge of the sprawling group there was one, very much larger den, which looked very different. It had dozens of twinkling torch-posts mounted along its front. What was more, it was most certainly occupied. From within, and also from a fenced-off section at its rear, they could hear the laughing growls and bellowing roars of bears having a rowdily good time. Benjamin and Mops crept closer.

'I can smell nut-doughs!' hissed Mops suddenly.

The mere mention of the word was enough to make Benjamin's mouth start watering. For a nut-dough – unlike other bear-foods, such as grated turnip root – tasted as delicious to a human as to a bear. It was made by mixing crushed beech nuts, hazel nuts and chestnuts into a soft sticky ball of dough, baking this ball over an open fire, then serving it piping hot and dripping with a layer of golden honey.

The smell also reminded Benjamin of just how hungry he was. As they'd made their way through Shadewell-Wood, he and Mops had been able to find sufficient wild fruits and berries to keep from starving, but certainly not enough to fill them completely.

They crept closer. The opening to a dark and narrow cobbled alley lay just a few paces away. Benjamin tiptoed across and peered in.

'Where do you think it leads, Mops?' he whispered.

'I shudder to think,' replied Mops.

The alley was grimy and littered with rubbish. At the far end they could just make out a solitary torch-post. But before then, beyond where the pale walls of the noisy den ended, a glow of light was spilling into the alley from above a stretch of high wooden fencing.

And not only light. In spite of her shudders, Mops

had ventured further into the alley. 'That nut-dough smell's definitely coming from down here,' she said, her nose twitching.

Without another word, she began to tip-toe along the rubbish-strewn cobbles to where the fence began. Benjamin followed, glancing anxiously over his shoulder to make sure that no bear was following *him*. By the time they reached the point where the stretch of fencing started, the smells had become even stronger. So too had the noise. From the other side of the fence, not only had the growls and roars grown louder, they'd grown fiercer. These were no longer the sounds of bears simply having a good time.

'What are they *doing* in there?' gasped Mops, as what sounded like a howl of torment rose above the roars.

Benjamin had no idea. Neither did he think it a good idea to stop and find out, enticing as the nut-dough smells were. The terrifying sounds coming from beyond the fence told him that the best thing they could do was leave – and quickly. So when, a short way ahead of him, Mops stopped at a gap in the fence and looked as if she was thinking of diving through, he hissed, 'Keep going!'

'I can't!'

'You've got to! Forget the nut-doughs, Mops. It's too dangerous to stay around here!'

'And I'm telling you I can't keep going!' squeaked Mops. 'Because there's a bear ahead!'

As she shrank back against the fence, Benjamin saw what she'd seen. In the pool of light cast by the single torch-post at the far end of the alley was the unmistakeable silhouette of a large, upright bear. It was facing sideways, one curved claw beckoning to some unseen companion.

'Back the way we came, Mops!' hissed Benjamin.

He turned, ready to run – only to stop. Another bear silhouette had appeared at that end of the alley too. This one was even more menacing for its silhouette showed that this bear was wielding a thick, club-like weapon.

'We're trapped!' cried Mops. 'What are we going to do now?'

Unusually for Mops, it was a silly question. There was only one thing they could do.

With a deep breath they dived through the gap in the fence and into the sea of noise and smells on the other side...

They found themselves behind two huge oak barrels, twice as tall as them and three times as wide. Benjamin and Mops were beautifully hidden (as was the hole in the broken fence, which explained why it hadn't been noticed and fixed before now). They risked a quick peep out and saw two long tubes snaking away from the barrels and across the grass. The end of one of the tubes had a slight leak in it, and a small puddle of liquid had formed on the ground near where they were crouching. It smelled truly awful.

'What is that stuff? hissed Mops, wrinkling her nose.

Benjamin knew. 'It's beer-drink.' He peered through the gap between the two barrels. 'And that must be a drinking-hole,' he pointed.

Mops took a look herself. The tube leading from the barrel ended at a hole in the ground. At least, she could only assume it was a hole. The edges weren't visible because the hole was overflowing with foam.

'You mean bears *drink* that stuff? And *live*?'

Benjamin nodded. 'My owner, Mrs Haggard, used to drink it sometimes. She'd come home smelling of it. And tottering from side to side.' He pointed. 'A bit like them!'

A couple of bears were waddling unsteadily towards the drinking-hole, laugh-growling as they went. A heavy, miserable-looking she-bear seemed to be guarding the hole. The two bears had to give her some payment before they were allowed to bury their snouts in the foam and begin slurping greedily.

'Up-time!' roared the hole-keeper after a little while.

Grumbling about being short-timed, the two drinkers lumbered off. The gap between the barrels wasn't wide enough for Benjamin and Mops to see where they went. They risked leaning around the side of one of the barrels. Not far, but far enough to see that they'd stumbled into a large, square, fenced-off area, thronged with noisy bears. And, in particular, to realise that they'd found out where the delicious nut-dough smells had been coming from.

The two drinker-bears had gone straight to where a short, sweating bear with a pair of tongs in his paw was standing beside a crackling fire. On a griddle laid across this fire were dozens of round balls of golden brown dough. The nut-dough seller finished serving a mean-looking bear holding a long stick. Then, in return for more money, he lifted two balls from the griddle, trickled honey over each, and handed them to the laugh-growling drinkers.

'What are these places?' hissed Mops. 'Did your Mrs Haggard ever say anything before she went out?'

(This question wasn't as odd as it might seem. It was well-known that bears talked to their human pets constantly, even though they didn't believe for one moment that they were being understood).

'Yes, she did sometimes,' said Benjamin. 'She'd say, 'Bum-fluff!' – that was one of the names she called me – 'Off-me to the sap-garden!''

'The *sap*-garden?' echoed Mops. 'Why call it that, when the place is only used by …'

She had been going to say 'bears'. And she would have done, had it not been for the terrible howl that suddenly came from the centre of the garden. For that howl – the same as they'd heard out in the alley – hadn't come from any bear. It could only have come, they now realised, from a sap: a human being. A human in torment.

Horrified by what they'd just heard, Benjamin and Mops risked leaning out further from their hiding place. In the very centre of the garden a group of bears were gathered in a circle. They were grunting and hooting fiercely. Suddenly, as that same awful howl rose again, the circle parted to show what was happening.

The mean-looking bear they'd seen being served with a nut-dough had stuck it onto the end of his long stick. He was now in the very centre of the bear circle. With him was a howling human.

The human was perhaps six or seven summers older than Benjamin, and strong, but it was clear he hadn't been fed for a good while. With his eyes fixed on the nut-dough as if it was the only thing in Bear Kingdom, he was leaping as high as he could to try and reach it.

'Jump, Roger Broadback!' the stick-holding bear was hollering.

But every time poor Roger Broadback jumped the stick was twitched out of reach, causing him to howl in anguish yet again.

'He's tiring,' said Benjamin.

In the centre of the bear circle Roger Broadback was now gasping for breath. He was still desperately trying to get hold of the nut-dough, but all the spring had gone out of his weary legs. The bear held his stick temptingly lower. With one final attempt Roger leapt – only for his fingers to fall tantalisingly short, as the tormenting bear knew they would. To a loud roar from those in the circle Roger Broadback collapsed in a heap, moaning pitifully.

Another bear stepped into the circle. He had a board on which the number 436 had been scratched. He held this aloft as he marched around the circle shouting, 'Roger Broadback, owner Ursus Covet, count-lasted four-three-six! Four-three-six! Bet-settle now!'

'That's disgraceful!' hissed Mops. 'They were trying to win money by guessing how long that poor Roger Broadback would keep on jumping before he collapsed!'

Around the circle, clinking coins were changing paws. None of them had come the way of Ursus Covet, though. Having roughly dragged the exhausted Roger Broadback to his feet, the angry bear was now hauling him across to the nearby fence.

'Lost-you me money-good,' Benjamin and Mops heard him snarl. 'Bet-me count-you-last five-hundred!'

Not far from their hiding place a strong length of rope hung from a hook embedded in a fence post. On reaching it, Ursus Covet looped this rope around Roger Broadback's waist and tied his hands behind his back. Then, as if wanting to be as cruel as he possibly could, the mean bear leaned the stick with its fragrant nut-dough right beside him.

With that, Ursus Covet turned back to the circle of bears. A loud burst of laugh-cheers had told him that the next event was about to begin. On the far side of the sap-garden, Benjamin saw another starving and wretched young human had been untied by his owner and was being thrust towards the waiting circle.

'Look, Mops,' hissed Benjamin, 'there are more!' He pointed towards the other humans he'd only just noticed, all tied to different parts of the sap-garden fence. 'Two over there, one in the corner, one right down at the end … Is that what a sap-garden really is, a place where humans are tormented just for fun?'

No answer.

'Mops?' He swung round. 'Mops! What are you doing!'

Mops hadn't answered his question for the simple reason that she hadn't heard it. She'd been crawling out from their hiding place on her hands and knees. As to what she was doing, Benjamin could see only too well. She was heading for the tied-up Roger Broadback. Or was she?

Mops had stopped at the long stick leaning against the fence. Still crouching on the ground, she now took hold of the end of the stick – and began moving it, not away from Roger Broadback as the tormenting Ursus Covet had done, but towards his mouth. The starving Roger, unable to believe his eyes as the nut-dough finally came his way, bit into with a loud cry of joy; a cry so loud and joyful that it could be heard above the excited babble of the circle of bears.

And heard it was, by Ursus Covet. Swinging round

from his place on the edge of the circle, Roger Broadback's owner was just in time to see his sap gulping down the nut-dough...and, still with the stick in her hands, the girl-sap who'd given it to him. With an angry roar, Ursus Covet began to lumber in Mops's direction.

Benjamin didn't hesitate. Leaping out from behind the barrels he raced over and grabbed Mops by the hand. 'Run!' he screeched.

In his panic, Benjamin completely forgot about the gap in the fence through which they'd got in to the sap-garden. Instead, he began to drag Mops towards the far end, hoping to find a way out there. They didn't reach it. The bears in the circle, their attention attracted by Ursus Covet's roar of rage, showed how quickly large bears can move if they need to. As Benjamin and Mops ran their way, they quickly strung themselves out right across their path. All the two friends could do was to skid to one side to avoid them.

But all that had done was to send them running into the very centre of the garden. The moment they did so the bear circle began to form again. They quickly found a solid wall of bears blocking the way ahead. They spun round...and round...and round...and stopped.

There was no longer any place for them to run to. The bears had formed their circle once again – and Benjamin and Mops were in the middle of it...

Also by **Michael Coleman**

£4.99

1 84362 183 5

'You scared Daniel?'
How many times has Tozer said that to me? Hundreds.

But this time it's different. We're not in school. He hasn't got me in a headlock, with one of his powerful fists wrenching my arm up, asking 'You scared, Weirdo?'

No. We're here, trapped underground together with no way out.

Shortlisted for the *Carnegie Medal, Lancashire Children's Book Award* and *Writers Guild Award*.

'Tense and psychological.' *The Times*

1 84362 299 8   £4.99

Luke is a thief who knows that crime *does* pay. Besides, what other way is there for someone like him?

Then he meets Jodi. She might be blind, but she can see where Luke's life is going wrong. And she has a burning ambition that only Luke can help her fulfil...if she can trust him.

So Luke decides to go straight. But when old acquaintances want to use his talents for one last job, can he resist? Or will he end up on the run again?

More Orchard Books

All priced at £4.99

Orchard Books are available from all good bookshops, or can be ordered direct from
the publisher: Orchard Books, PO BOX 29, Douglas IM99 1BQ
Credit card orders please telephone 01624 836000
or fax 01624 837033 or visit our Internet site: www.wattspub.co.uk
or e-mail: bookshop@enterprise.net for details.

To order please quote title, author and ISBN
and your full name and address.
Cheques and postal orders should be made payable to 'Bookpost plc.'
Postage and packing is FREE within the UK
(overseas customers should add £1.00 per book).

Prices and availability are subject to change.